THE ALMIGHTY GOAT AND POEMS

Dr. N S. Lajevardi

GoToPublish LLC
1-888-337-1724
www.gotopublish.com
info@gotopublish.com

CONTENTS

Hardware Barbershop..1
Funs 5
Group Hug 11
Guilty Man (Condemned Man) 19
The Almighty Goat 25
Portrait of Homer...29
Story of Her Life 35
Teacher of "Seven Heaven" School................................41
The Daddy's Ears 49
The Sale of a House 53
The Secret of My Uncles 59
Thus Spoke Minestrone 65
The Hell "Jell" 69
POEMS 78
Oneness 79
Pledge of Union...80
Paraphrase translation of a Rumi Sonnet (Ghazal) 81
Translation of Rumi's souls ' evolution By: N. S. L........82
Translation of some Rumi's Rubaii 83
Another Rumi's translation by N.S.L 84
Rūmi's Rubaï traduit en francais 84
Il mio Sonetto in French 84
The opera of the Jungle 85

To whom thinking is Pleasure and
Doubt is Belief and
Knowledge is Heaven . . .

To My Family

HARDWARE BARBERSHOP

A man entered a barbershop and asked for sandpaper. The barbershop owner looked at him and then to his assistant. While stunned by the question, he replied "Sandpaper?"

"Yes"

"You know, we are a barbershop and we have also skin care lotions, manicure and pedicure supplies. That is it. Yes, we also have shampoo, gels and of course, hair supplies."

"You know sir, I want the sandpaper for the soles of my feet and around my toes which are badly corned, that's why I would consider the sandpaper a skin care product."

"Oh yes, you're right. We will order it and you'll get it next time." The man left and the barber told his assistant about the idea of providing whatever is necessary for skin care. He got out and bought some sandpaper and on the window of his shop he added, "We now have sandpaper for tough skin."

The day after, another man came in and asked if they carried plywood.

"Plywood?"

"Yes."

He looked again at his assistant and with open eyes and lips, showed his surprise. The assistant, looking at the new arrival, said: "I don't know."

The barber replied to the man "I understand; you want it for skin improvement, right?"

"Actually . . ."

The barber cut off his sentence and said: "You can separate different layers and apply it."

"Sort of."

"No, I am sorry; we don't have it but the next time you come we will have it." The customer left and the barber turned his eyes toward his assistant and said: "Once again, another skin care product that we don't have."

"What?"

"What?! What?!"

"Plywood and skin?"

"You don't understand. I don't understand either. They know how to apply it on their skin and you're better to shut up."

"Listen boss . . ."

"Don't do listen. We don't know what the new market is. Don't you know that every day they are talking about the craziness of the stock market?

Do you understand that? Of course not, me neither"

"But."

"No buts, go and ask for a few small sized pieces of plywood." Now another sign on the window: "Plywood"

The same day an old customer walked in. His arthritis was painful that day, maybe because of the low barometric pressure and rain in the forecast. He sat down and he saw the plywood. He looked at the barber and then at his assistant and while replacing his dentures in his mouth said: "Are you doing some renovation and reconstruction work?" "Yes," said the barber.

"Good for you. It's good for the business to have new ideas."

The barber looked at his assistant and said: "Didn't I tell you? You always need new ideas." Then he got started to trim his customer's hair and asked him whether he needed some sandpaper to depeel his feet's skin.

"Oh yes, as a matter of fact I need some."

"How about plywood?"

"No, no, I'll be OK with the sandpaper." The poor man did not know how to use the plywood on his mustache or his hair, or his skin, or his toes, and he did not ask for anything more. He left the barber shop and the owner looked at his assistant while he raised his eyebrow and had a smile of victory.

As soon as the customer left, a lady walked in. The barber was surprised to see a lady in his shop and his assistant went to the lady and asked: "How can

I help you?"

"I need some plywood, a couple of pieces of sandpaper and a shampoo for oily hair." The assistant helped her out and got the many and said,

"Anything else today?"

"As a matter of fact, I need a screwdriver, do you have any?"

"I am sorry, not yet, but we'll have some pretty soon." replied the barber, and said to his assistant: "Remember to purchase that."

"Screwdriver?"

"I told you no questions."

"OK, sir."

The lady left and the barber said to his assistant: "If your hair and skin care device get lost and you need to fix them, where you get 'em?"

"In a hardware store."

"Wrong. In a barber shop. That is the answer."

"If people come and ask about 'drain clog fluid', then what?"

"Let me ask you a question."

"Please, do."

"Have you heard that iron is necessary for blood and blood brings nutritional material to the skin?" The assistant looked at his boss while doubting about the question and the answer and opened his mouth to answer, but the boss didn't let him reply and added "So if you need iron, the logic says that you've got to go to a beauty salon, to a barber shop."

"But . . ."

"No buts, we have to follow people's demands."

"We are barber shop people."

"No, we are ahead-of-time-barbers who know the law of supply and demand."

"Supply and what?"

"Never mind. Go back to your work."

The assistant returned back to his work: to make room for new supplies, and the barber went to the telephone directory looking after "screwdriver suppliers".

Two other customers came in and both men requested to get their hair cut. The older one said "Hello" and then said, "How are you doing?"

"Long time no see, man," said the barber.

The other customer, a young man, without saying hello, or good afternoon, got in the chair and asked for a short haircut and closed his eyes as he was about to sleep.

"I see you're developing your business," said the older customer.

"Yes. The law of supply and demand. By the way, how is your wife?"

"You said it. She is very demanding. By the way, give me a trim and trim my mustache."

"OK, you will get it as usual."

"What?"

"I said as usual."

"Yes, my wife is as usual, demanding, but very careful about my mustache."

"What, what do you mean?"

"I said be careful with my wife. I mean with my mustache."

The barber laughed and looked at his assistant while smiling and pointing at the customer's ear. Meanwhile the young customer opened his eyes and with his eye opened screamed, "Why did you give me a short haircut?"

"You asked for it."

"No, what I meant was short in the front but left alone in the back."

"The back side needed it."

"Do what I am telling you, man. You understand, man?"

"You did not say that?"

"Are you crazy? Don't you see that I look like a jerk now?"

"I am sorry, be my guest and don't pay."

"Next time, remember that. Otherwise, I'll sue you."

"OK man. Have a good day." The assistant was so scared and the young customer asked for a box of screwdrivers. He got that and did not pay for it as the boss intervened and gave it to him as a gift. The boy left and the boss looked angrily at his assistant.

The assistant said: "What? He asked for a short haircut."

"I know. I was angry at him. I want to tell you how the screwdriver saved our butts."

"You're right, Sir."

The old customer came into this conversation and said: "What screw?

Who got screwed? Isn't it my mustache?"

"Nothing, no, your mustache is all right and everything is just fine."

"How much?"

"As usual."

"It was two dollars right?"

"No it was twelve dollars."

The old customer gave a ten dollar bill and said: "Keep the change."

"Thank you. Don't you want some skin care products for your wife?"

By the way, give a sandpaper piece for my wife's tongue." He got the sandpaper, paid for it and said, "See you soon." "See you," replied the assistant.

In a short period of time the barbershop became a successful postmodern: "Hardware Store with Consultant Barbershop".

FUNS

"Grandma "asked Désireh, a teenager, "are we born to have fun?" The grandma, Sweet, who was not that old and for sure she could have been at most a mom, replied, "Oh, yeah." And she went back to her cigarette and her beer can, and while cracking her gum a few times she said: "You know we are born to have fun. God has created all other creatures and all other things for our pleasure to serve."

"Is your pleasure the same as other people?" asked Désireh.

"Oh yeah."

"You mean if you smoke I have to have fun with it?"

"If you don't, you can go out and get busy with other pleasures. That is why there are so many pleasures out there."

"I want to get married."

"Now?"

"Yeah, why not?"

"You have to wait a little bit, and on the other hand a husband is a sort of annoying creature. As I told you, everything is created by God for our pleasure."

"Even husbands?"

"Yeah."

"Why wait if the pleasure is out there waiting for us?"

"This is a good question. In reality I don't want your pleasure to interfere with your mind."

"What are you saying?"

"What I am saying is first get a boyfriend. You have him in your mind while you try another one. You get now both of them in mind and you go for the third one."

"Wait a minute grandma, don't you think if you go to the second one, the first one will get hurt and will go away and will not accept your polygamy?"

"Don't worry. He will do the same thing. As long as they have fun, they don't bother to deal with unfaithfulness."

"At what age can you have a boyfriend?"

"As soon as you're ready. It's like meat and teeth. You have teeth, you're ready to eat meat."

"On the other hand, what do I need a boyfriend for? This is nothing but trouble. The only thing I need is their money. They have to put money into this relationship. Right Grandma?"

"Yes. As I told you, when you have the teeth you can have them. You are mature as soon as you can be part of the 'supply and demand'."

"What do I have to tell to others?"

"Listen Sweety, (she was always called by this nickname) I have to go out. I have a date, and your mom will come back pretty soon with the dinner. So you can practice a little bit your dance and song and we will discuss this matter tomorrow."

"OK Grandma."

Grandma left and Sweety went outside to socialize with her friends and to practice her dance and their songs.

An old man was sitting on his porch. He was smoking and singing quietly an old song. The song was about the river, and the canyon:

One was destroying the other one while shaping it.

The other one was nourishing the first one with his springs.

The river's source was the canyon's springs

The river was eroding the Canyon in order to get more water.

The kids were at once amazed by the song and wanted to know the meaning of the lyrics. They went to the old man who looked awful and cautiously asked him about the song and the lyrics. He puffed his cigarette with a strong inhalation and said, "If you want me to give you something, you have to give me something."

"What do you want Grandpa?" asked one of the kids.

"Anything at all."

"How about a kiss?" the other kid asked.

"That'll do it."

"No, I have a better idea." said Sweety. "I will bring you a can of beer of my mom's."

"It's even better." said the old man.

Sweety, at once went back home and came back with a cold can of beer.

The old man drank the beer in one gulp and looked at the kids and said, "You know, I mean, the meaning of those lyrics is, I mean, like a gardener who is trimming the vineyard and shaping the trees at the best exposure to light and, I mean, why he is doing that?"

"To make it better." replied all the kids, "But this has nothing to do with the river."

"Oh yeah? I mean, if you think, you know what I mean. You will see the goal of the gardener is to extract and distill the soul of the vineyard, which is the vine. Better vine. You see what I mean? The river does the same thing." "I don't get you," says one of the kids.

"I don't care." said Sweety. "I don't care about all that stuff. This is not part of supply and demand."

"What are you talking about?" said the old man.

"My grandma says, don't bother with those people, live your life, enjoy it and have fun. If others are dying, that is their problem. And she says . . ." "Is there any sense of humanity in her comment?" says the old man.

"Let us play and leave him alone," said a girl.

They went back to their fun and left the old man in his world.

"Your mom is coming, Sweety," said one of the girls.

Sweety looked back and saw her mom coming with a man called Aron. The couple went to the house and Sweety followed them. "Where is the dinner mom?"

"What dinner? You did not eat your dinner yet?" replied mom.

"No, grandma said you will bring something for dinner."

"Why didn't you call me?"

"Grandma said, don't call your mom. She is busy. I mean, I was like . . ."

"You stupid girl, you've got to use your damn brain."

"Excuse me," she replied with a special tone that was like, "You! Mindless mom, you have to take care of your children instead of taking care of your pleasures".

"Go and buy something for yourself and for us."

"Like what?"

"Anything."

"Give me money."

Aron gave her a ten-dollar bill and she went out to shop.

At the corner of the street a 7-11 market had opened very recently. The manager was very nice and educated man. He was handling the business with his wife.

"Can you give me something for dinner?" asked Sweety when she got to the 7-11 market.

"Wait a minute 'til we finish with two customers, "replied the manager's wife.

"OK," said Sweety.

"OK, now, what do you want?" asked the husband.

"Something good for dinner."

"How much money you want to spend?"

"Ten dollars."

"Ok, I am going to give you a pack of hot dogs with rolls of whole wheat bread, and an orange juice, ketchup and a pack of peanuts."

"I don't want orange juice, give me ..."

"No, orange juice is better than any of these soft drinks."

"Can you give me beer instead?"

"No. Orange juice as I said."

"Ok, man, whatever," she said.

She got the food and went back home. She put the hot dogs in the microwave and a pack of six was enough for three of them, with plenty of tomato ketchup.

"Dinner is ready," she screamed.

"OK, we'll be there right away."

They got their food and at the same time grandma got back home with a man called Sharon. Sharon and Aron were twin brothers. Grandma went to the bathroom while leaving Sharon with the others.

In the living room, Aron asked "Sharon, how're you doing?"

"Good, no complaints."

"Are you having fun?"

"Yes, how about yourself?"

"Oh yeah."

"Have you eaten yet?"

"No, we're about to have our dinner, you can join us." He looked at his brother as if to say, I am kidding.

"Are you kidding me?"

"No, you can share my food."

"Can I?"

"You know, you remind me a man who was eating a small fried leg of frog. His brother asked him whether he can give him a bit. The man gave him the frog leg and said "Now you give me a bit of that." It's already a bit and he got the bit back." Everybody laughed.

"I got you. OK. We are not going to share your food." said Sharon. "Have fun. Bon appetit."

Sweety was following the conversation between brothers and when the grandma got back from the bathroom she went to her and said "You said that we are, the ones who are supposed to have fun, but these guys are talking about "fun". What is going on?"

"You know, they can talk as much as they want, this is a free country. As long as they are in the frame of 'demand-supply', they're OK." "I don't get you," said Sweety, "What supply?" "Supply of goods," said Grandma.

"Of very good ones," said Aron and everybody laughed.

"Not as good as your daughter," said Sharon.

"Excuse me," said Grandma.

"Watch out!" said Aron.

Sweety was almost on the track of understanding, but somehow she was a bit confused and said "How about "demand?".

"In a global economy we speculate the demand. There is no real demand. This is just an illusion, "said grandma.

"What?" said Aron with wide open eyes. He made a coordinated smooth move with both his head and hands like a little dance of disbelief.

"We are all the customers of your goods," said Sharon.

"Of your very good goods," said Aron.

"Not really. You think you are needy; we forced you to believe that you need to consume. And when you get used to it, we will control the market. Even at this moment Sweety is ready for the market of fun but we have to see what the demand-supply function is in order to have the highest profit"

Sweety came to the rescue and said, "We have to encourage men to consume and to persuade them that a free country is where there is a free market. You can buy what you desire. No government control at all." "You can also buy the government." said grandma.

"Bravo," said Aron.

"Bravo to who?" said Sharon while looking at Aron.

Aron waited for a while and said "To both, mother and daughter."

Sweety said angrily, "What about me?"

"I said mothers and daughter," said Aron.

"No you said mother and daughter," said Sharon.

"I meant all mothers and all daughters' financial institution."

"OK. Apology is accepted," said Sweety, and she continued "Now, could I get into the market of fun?"

"If you can separate 'fun' from 'humanism', yes," replied Grandma.

"Once again?" said Sweety.

"There is no humanism in my market. Market is not a place for virtue and passion. You have to turn your attention, the radios, TV and everything related to bad news, back to the fun track. And remember, we are born to have fun and to consume and we don't care about the rest of the world. You got that?"

"Yes I did," said Sweety.

"Let us celebrate that," said Grandma, while going to the fridge for a can of beer.

"There is no more beer in the fridge," said Désireh.

"Go to the old man of next door, he has plenty," said Sweety.

"Never mind. He wants to destroy 'the perishable environment' and I don't like it," said Grandma, "I will celebrate that with 'marijuana'."

"I love her," said Aron.

"Me too," said Sharon.

"Excuse me?" said Sweety with a gyration like a belly dancer, swinging her hips and waving her hands.

"Me too," said Sweety's mom.

"What?" Everybody looked at her with stunned faces.

"What? Why are you so stunned? Am I good at it, too, or what?" Mom said while doing her own version of Sweety's bump and grind.

"You're good at everything else but not at that." said Sharon.

"No. What I mean is to get the conversation back to more interesting tracks." she said.

"Like what we can to tonight?"

"All right, let us forget about tomorrow and all the rests and celebrate the moment," said Sharon while everybody sat down for a very weak dinner.

GROUP HUG

Ms O's secretary got the phone and answers. "Hello, how can I help you out?"

"Hello. Good morning. Is this Ms O's office?"

"Yes Madame," she says carefully.

"In connection with your daily show, I've a concern. I mean I have a request."

"What kind of concern Madame?" She listened cautiously, frowning slightly with her fingertips touching at a forty five degree angle, her eyes wide and alert.

"You know, nothing really very important, but very important for me and my family. By the way my name is Mrs. Y. Y ..."

"What is going on Madame Y.?"

"I happened to know a gentleman—the very real father of my children— fifty years ago. Unfortunately he doesn't know he is the father of my children and I want you, I am begging you, rather, to find him and to get him on your show and have him face the fact."

"Oh Madame, could you please, hold on a minute?"

"Yes of course. Take your time." She now had a smile on her face.

The secretary got connected to the manager and the manager to the general manager and the general manager to the assistant producer and the later to the lady show producer. She was told about the case which was as old as half a century. She gave a green light for getting involved with the case and her agreement went back to the secretary via the ladder of hierarchy. The secretary got back to the phone and asked about the identification of the man called Mr. X.

"As far as I know he is an OB/Gyn Dr. living in Canada with his family."

"OK Mrs. Y. We'll call you if we get positive reactions from the other side. Meanwhile let me please have your phone number and your e-mail address and hang on."

Mrs. Y was about 70 years old, still a pretty woman with grey hair and a very distinguished manner. Her husband had left a good fortune for his wife and the twin boys who are now over forty years old living with her in their California vineyard of one thousand acres. They have a line of wine production of prime quality. One of the boys is the manager of the vineyard and the other one is the manager of the wine production. Both of them graduated from the University of California at Davis. They are married. The first has two boys and the second has three daughters.

Time passed by and the office of Mrs. O got very involved with this fascinating case. As a matter of fact, the secretary was sent to Canada. She got an appointment, as a patient, with Dr. X. As the day of visit approached the secretary was much excited. Finally she found herself in a very luxurious office and ready to be examined by Dr. X. A tall man with grey hair, brown eyes and a beautiful smile, approached her looking like an angel, shook her hand and said, "What brings you here Mrs. S?"

The secretary, Mrs. S was astonished by the deeps scrutiny of Dr. X. She did not get his question at first and like a checkmated king couldn't move. "Is something bothering you Mrs. S.?"

"Ah, no, not at all. In fact I am not sick at all."

"Why are you here, then?" asked Dr. X.

"You know Dr. X, a lady called us and . . ."

"Us, what do you mean us?"

"The office of Ms. O. you know." She was at a loss for words, even though she was very apt and reliable secretary.

"Oh, yes, how is she doing?"

"Ms O.?"

"Yes."

"She is doing great. I was telling you about a lady called, Mrs. Y . . . She is assuming that you're the father of her twins, and she wants you to be on

Ms. O.'s show."

"How old is this lady?" He narrowed his eyes and frowned slightly.

"She is seventy and a bit strong."

"You mean fat?"

"I wouldn't say so. But she is not slim, for sure." Then, as the secretary was in the specialist's office she took advantage of it and dealt with some feminine issues and got a prescription.

Dr. X meanwhile agreed to go on Ms. O's show.

One month later, Ms. O. was on stage. The audience selected for this special show applauded and welcomed Ms. O. All the ladies of the audience had successful lives, distinguished backgrounds and came from well off families. They were invited to observe the dialogue between the two old partners. For the audience there were the inducements of a party and the offer of an automobile by the producer, the party to be supplied by different sponsoring firms and advertising corporations. Mrs. Y has also promised to bring enough cases of her wines for all the audience.

Ms O starts to introduce Mrs. Y.Y. What we see is a nice and beautiful old lady, who seems to be a very good mother and a very faithful wife.

"Mrs. Y. what is going on? What was your relationship with Dr. X?"

"I was about twenty and got married to my husband Mr. Y. We were neighbors in the wine valley and our vineyard was managed by my father who was a good friend of my husband's father. This was the beginning of wine production in California. Our wedding was superb and everything was in my favor."

"You mean you planned your wedding yourself?" asked Ms. O ...

"Yes." replied Mrs. Y. Y ... The audience was nothing but ears, but of course, from time to time, like now, they had to break to commercials. After that Mrs. Y. Y. added, "After a few months of marriage we learned that we can't have babies. We decided to adopt one." "What a good idea," said Ms O ...

"Yes, that was a good idea. All things considered by my husband, Europe was the place to go to find a baby. My husband asked me to go and see what I could do. I went to Europe but the more I tried the less I was successful. My husband and I decided to get divorced and to remarry someone else to see if we can have our own lives and our own babies."

"It was so important that you have decided to destroy your nest of love?" asked Ms. O ...

"You know, in our communities the goal of marriage is to have children." replied Mrs. Y. Y ...

"Isn't it a bit strange?"

"Not for our milieu. Especially after we had a good deal of consultation with parents, friends, our church authorities and our party."

"What did your party have to do with your life?" said Ms. O.

"You know Ms. O, you can't deny the role corporations play in your beliefs and political direction."

"Please go ahead," replied Ms. O, while showing signs of disagreement.

"Anyway we decided to go on and follow our separate destiny."

"You mean destiny dictated by corporations?"

"Sort of," said Mrs. Y. Y. and continues. "I went back to France for some advice for wine production problems. It was the 14th of July and in each square and circle people were dancing with live music. I was in the Place de la Sorbonne, in a small plaza in front of the old university. I took a chair behind a table. The waiter came and I asked for a glass of red wine. I was fat much fatter than today."

"You're not fat." said Ms. O., while smiling and looking at the audience.

"Thank you for the compliment." She replied and continued, "I was very active, very lively. My French was awful and my dress was ridicule." "You mean ridiculous.", said Ms. O., smiling.

"Yes, and somehow too casual."

The waiter brought my glass of wine, and all of a sudden on the other side of the pavement a boy who was looking at me smiled and came toward my table. He was beautiful, with wide brown eyes and dark hair and was very well dressed. He was slim but very well-built like one of those Greek Gods from the sky. He came and all of a sudden my glass of wine got broken on the pavement.

"An act of God, a miracle." Said Ms. O. The audience laughed.

"No, my clumsiness." said Mrs. Y. Y … "Anyway, he came over to me and, in French, asked me whether he could help me out. We got into conversation and then a bottle of wine and we were dancing and laughing. He was almost my age and he invited me to his place."

"Oh, oh." replied Ms. O., laughing again.

Mrs. Y. Y. shook her head and continued, "It was almost morning that we went to his place. The only thing I remember was that we were together for three consecutive days; living on tuna, bread, coffee, fruit and old baguettes."

"Ooh la la." said Ms. O. and everybody laughed.

"After that we went out to buy some food."

"You didn't need it, did you?" and there was more laughter.

"Then I realized that my flight was the same day in almost two hours."

"You didn't need it, you were already flying, right?" replied Ms. O., still laughing.

"You know, business is business."

"The corporation's influence," said Ms. O.

"I don't know. He went out to get money from his saving account and I was confused. I went back to my hotel. I packed in few minutes and at the right time I was in the plane. Even though his face and his smile were everywhere, even in my luggage. He was inside me. My heart was divided between him and my old husband. The plane flew toward NY and my eyes, while open, were seeing two images in one screen, my old husband and Mr. X. Eventually, I got back home to my vineyard, very tired and exhausted."

"What happened to the clues to solve your problems of wine production?"

"What are you talking about? I was in Paris but most of the time in bed." At this the audience laughed again. She turned her face to them and looked pointedly at her twins and said: "They were the clue.", at which everyone applauded.

Ms. O., fascinated by the story, asked: "Then what happened to Dr. X. and …"

Mrs. Y. Y. cut her off. "When I became pregnant my old husband came back and asked me to marry him, "she replied and continued, "We got back together and our children got born and I was curious to know what had happened to the real father. Back and forth, without being noticed, I've found out that he graduated from medical school in France and is established in Canada and with his own clinic."

"Do you have the FBI in your service?" said Ms. O., laughing.

"If we want to know something, we women, we can find it out, right?" said Mrs. Y. Y. and continued, "He is married, happily married and has two sets of twins, two boys and two girls."

"It seems he has a gene for that." said Ms. O. laughing some more. "You had better go back stage to the waiting room while we introduce Dr. X to the audience."

"OK, see you soon. Don't forget me in there." At this the audience laughed again, too.

Mrs. Y. Y. went backstage and within two minutes, after the commercial break, Dr. X. came on stage with Ms. O … A deep silence roofed the studio and the audience. Even Ms. O. was speechless for some time as Dr. X. walked toward her, a bit tired from the trip but joyful. A man walking like a real god who is trying to persuade his people with his eminent presence. He sat down and asked Ms. O. to sit down, something which was completely the contrary of how it was usually done with Ms.O.

"Dr. X., do you remember this lady?" asked Ms. O. while a recent picture of Mrs. Y. Y. was projected.

Dr. X. was looking at the picture and then turned back to the audience. His eyes, suddenly, were fixed on the middle-aged twin boys sitting there. He looked back to the picture, then once again back to the boys and finally said, "I have during last 50 years seen and met almost 10, 000 women." People were amazed.

"What?" said Ms. O., stunned.

"Yes, three to four hundred patients for every year and over forty five years of practice. You can make the calculation yourself. Of course some were regular patients for a long period of time. That is why ten thousand is a good number."

"You're right." said Ms. O., "but you did not answer my question."

He got up and went toward the twins, wordlessly, with tears his eyes. He opened his arms, took a long deep breath and said, "I know you. You're my blood." He turned back to look at Ms. O. "I was only 17 year old when I met her."

"You mean she had a love experience with a minor."

"No, no, I was already mature. I had started college when I met her and I was financially and spiritually on my own. What is maturity all about? Is it a number or is it manner, behavior, feeling, responsibility?" All the audience was applauding and at the same time crying.

"You're right sir." said Ms. O . . . "There are whole lots of people who have years and age but not maturity."

"Your mother left me without leaving a note. I am sure that she had a reason for her bizarre action. I don't blame her. God knows that I was looking for her for several months. I had no possibility to go after her to America and then I found another love whom I married."

"Do you want to see her?"

"I would love to." He was holding the twins' hands and shaking them as though asking their agreement. People applauded for a minute or so and at the same time Mrs. Y. Y. came onto the stage with tears in her eyes.

The audience witnessed Dr. X. leaving the twins and coming back on the stage with his arms still open. He and Mrs. Y. Y. hugged each other for a minute and then boys also came on the stage. There was another hug and kisses and tears of joy, showing love and affection from all sides.

"Do you have any complaints Dr. X.?" asked Ms. O . . .

"Not at all. That was an old issue and I understand her family's point of view and once again I am a happy man who is blessed with his family members."

In the audience there were tears and applause.

"I am happy to see the reunion of two families." said Ms. O ... She asked the grandchildren and their mothers, who were in the audience also, to the stage, and then there was an even bigger group hug.

Dr. X. with tears in his eyes faced the audience and said, "I've heard that you are going to get a gift from the show sponsoring this event. But for me the best event in my entire life is to see my neighbor happy. My neighbor is now in Africa, in Asia, in South America without food and without medicine and O., I am ready to give 2.5 million to the U.N. for this matter. Each member of the Y. family also has promised to give the same amount of money."

Ms. O. said: "OK, instead of giving away a car to this audience of 200 persons we will give money to the U.N. for this purpose and as for me I will match the same amount."

The audience of rich people also committed itself to the same amount of money.

Together, almost 200 million for poor people was raised in one show.

"This was a good show!" said Ms. O.

"If there is justice, fairness and peace in the world, the hate and evil doing will disappear," said Dr. X ...

"Let us have a group hug with the people of the world. "said Ms. O. while the show ended.

GUILTY MAN (CONDEMNED MAN)

A man in an ancient dark age time was sentenced to death. He was a dark faced short man with curly hair and a glance at his face and features was good enough to tell that his was not chosen by God. He allegedly claimed it was his land and his property which was occupied by the Emperor's soldiers for its underground treasures. As the matter of fact all underground and any land was given to the Emperor by a decree of God.

The Emperor was the Image of God on the earth, with blue eyes and a perfect body and fair complexion, which are good enough to prove his divine messenger status.

This guilty man of a non-believer-tribe was living in this land for centuries and way back the cattle of his ancestors were taken by the same Dynasty of Kings and by another God's decree, while eliminating all aspects of his culture and traditions. No question at all. That was an act of God. Then the men of this tribe started, for living, to lay bricks and dry them in sun and setting them for fortification of soldier's trenches.

Anyway, that man was sent to the cage of a hungry and angry lion. The lion was the most powerful creature of God and of course in the service of the Emperor.

The man, one of «the domesticated animals» as the Emperor used to call them, in a corner of the cage, was looking miserably at the lion. The beautiful lion with a jump gets to the man's corner and the man, horrified, yelled "Hush". The lion, for a second was distracted, and then when it grabbed the man's neck, heard the man was trying to tell him something.

The lion said, "What? Are you praying? Aren't you supposed to be a non-believer?"

"Hush, listen!"

"You don't have to talk; this is the divine Scripture code."

"What do you mean?" the agonized man replied, while choking and coughing.

"The divine Scripture says that the ordinary men don't talk, don't have cognition, and don't have ideas and intuition. They just follow the divine

Rules." Out of the corners of his eyes, the lion looked at the Emperor.

"I know that. I wanted to tell you something very important." He coughed and coughed and couldn't continue.

"OK, do it fast."

The man said something while held down by the lion. The lion released the man and with his tale between his legs and head down left the cage while mumbling to himself something no one could understand and spitting on the ground.

The Emperor and his entourage were astonished, looking at each other with eyes and mouth open. They were sitting in the Royal Box of the Stadium and wanted justice to be done. One of the Consuls who was the Secretary of Ethic went to the Emperor to give his testimony.

He too was a man with dark and curly hair. In those days this king, complexion and hair was a controversy. The source of this controversy was as follows

"According to Scripture a man with curly hair went for the last judgment.

The Angel who was in charge of the Heaven's gate was blind. He did not like curly hair and used to touch people's hair. If the hair of new arrivals to the gate was curly, the angel used to send them right away to Hell, and if the hair was straight he sent them right to Heaven.

The curly haired man knew this "judgment". He was waiting his turn in order to get sent to either Hell, or to Heaven. He got a good idea and when his turn came up he approached the Angel, step by step while putting his weight on each leg and looking at him with half closed eyes. He then took off his pants and then his underwear. He did a hand stand with his butt toward the face of the Angel. The Angel touched his butt. The butt was soft and had no curly hair, and after this examination the Angel said "Good boy, welcome to Heaven."

The man ran to the gate as soon as he got back on his feet, but the Angel called him. The curly haired man stopped and was scared at his death, his second death. He said to himself, while tying his pants "That is it. He found out my trick."

"Hey," said the Angel "come back!"

"Yes Sir. What is up?"

"Listen, my man. I am glad you're a war veteran with a large injury on the scalp. War against non-believers is divine, it's wonderful, but you know, my man, your mouth stinks. Take this chewing gum and get rid of that shit-smelling mouth."

The curly haired man escaped safe and sound but still the society was "stinky-mouth-curly-hair-man kind of race." judgmental about them as a people.

Anyway, the Consul went to the Emperor. The Emperor said, "Didn't I tell you to get a very short hair cut?"

"Yes my Lord, you did."

"Why the hell didn't you do it?"

"Because my wife was using the razor blade for her leg hair and she was your date last night."

The Emperor looked at him with admiration and then looked to the other side and said, "Yeah, OK. What did you want to say?"

"We have to change our lion."

"What?" screamed the Emperor "Are you out of you mind? Our lion is very sophisticated and has a very intelligent attack."

"But . . ."

"No but." His righthand finger was pointing up in the air and he continued "We have to know what happened with the guilty man and why the lion gave up eating him. I knew that the flesh and the skin of curly haired persons is bitter." He shook his head and stuck out his tongue.

"Yes my Lord," said the Consul of Ethic Affairs and went for inquiries. He went to the condemned man and said "What happened? What is wrong with you? Damn it!"

"What is wrong with me or with your lion?"

"Nothing is wrong with the lion. If you don't say the truth, God damn it, we will get your pants off and you'll be ashamed of yourself for the rest of your life because of getting exposed nude to the public. You like it? The truth or else!"

"Am I spared of death penalty if I say the truth?"

"Yes, of course," and he shook his head up and down.

"OK. Get me to the Emperor. I'll tell him what happened myself."

"Let us go."

The consul brought the man to the Emperor. The Emperor, with eyes like an angry dog and the mouth of a demon while shaking his head and pointing his finger at him said "What happened? Why did the lion not devour you?"

"He did not like my flesh."

"Don't lie!» said the Consul and he turned the head toward the Emperor and while bending and touching his head to the ground, said, "He said something to the lion, my Lord, that's why the lion did not eat him."

"Are you going to tell us your secret? You'd better or else," said the Emperor.

"Yes, my Lord, but first you have to promise to spare my life."

"Nonsense," said the Emperor while showing a ridiculing smile and shaking his head. He looked to the Consul and said "You give your razor blade to your daughter and . . ."

"She is not yet fourteen, and . . ."

"Shut up," and the Emperor turned the head toward the condemned man and said "OK, on one condition, no more talk about your heritage and your land."

"OK, as you wish my Seignior."

"My Lord! Watch your language," said the Emperor.

"OK my Lord."

The Emperor tried to see his horoscope in his rosary. His rosary was made of royal farm goat's dung droppings. Some noble people specialized in making it into beads and putting one after the other on a silk thread. While doing so they have to recall Emperor's ancestors' names and while reciting their names they have to bend their head in order to show their respect for the divine dynasty.

A glaze of gold then garnishes the rosary.

For the lower level people the donkey's dung was first pressed and with a water spray the dropping is made like a sphere or bullet and then dried and finally put on the rosary.

The high priest has one of these but made of female donkey's dung. According to the royal medical association, inhalation of the smoke of this last dung, when burnt, was a remedy for chest pain, stress, skin acnes and encouraged mustache and hair growth. For this reason the whole city was smelling like a burnt animal stable.

The Emperor had a rosary of one hundred round and uniform spheres of goat dung. And from time to time according to a decision making situation, he would hold one end of the rosary with two fingers of one hand and with closed eyes he grabbed at random with two fingers of the other hand another place on the rosary then he counted the number of spheres between the two sets of fingers. If the number of spheres are very close to ten or some number times ten the decision made is good, otherwise far from ten, the worst the decision.

That was the source of policies in the city and of course the Chief Astrologist was always present. The Chief Astrologist was present and the Emperor had decided to give clemency to the curly haired man and a piece of burnt female donkey shit also was, every time, burnt close to the nose of the Emperor for the healing power. Later on with more civilized societies that was replaced by dog shit because of better healing power.

Anyway, the Emperor, after couple of good inhalations of burnt shit, while closing and opening his eyes and bringing some smoke toward his mustache with his hands said "OK. You will be released as I promised with the condition that was mentioned before and tell me your secret now."

"My Lord, your majesty, I was agonizing and for my last free speech, granted by lion, I told him "You may eat me, but remember the new traditions, you have to write a short story and read it in front of the majesty. The lion hated short stories and speech and left the battle ground."

THE ALMIGHTY GOAT

A man had a billy goat with a champion background, good genes, high yield, long lasting life, hardy for winter and hot weather. He lived on such a low diet, he was able to eat everything, even old newspapers like the Sunday Times with all kinds of colors and advertisements. He was very friendly and good sprinter. By that, I mean the goat was good for coupling and transferring the best of his genes.

Every day, from all over the country, as far as two hundred miles, breeders and farmers brought their goats, female ones, to get some of the good genes and spread it to their next generations. How many kids had our champion? God knows it. A good army of good genes. That poor champion was very humble. He never questioned his master, no "Why?", no "Ouch!", no "Sigh!". In that respect our champion had some gene from some donkey, I believe. He was a very trustful genre of person. He believes whatever the master says. If the master says, for instance, "Donkey flies and sings like a mocking bird.", our champion would say "Of course donkey flies.", especially because donkey was one of the ancestors of our champion. I don't know how he got the gene from that animal, but he got it by the will of the Master, in the cave of Plato. You can transform any 3D person into 2D or 4D into 2D. Another thing which was very peculiar about that "goat, the champion", was the fact that he believes his Master has a good connection with Gods, or with the selected Race. Don't tell me that freemasons have something to do with that because our billy goat is sort of homeless person.

Anyway, one evening after a long and hard working day for the master and for the champion, the company got finally a rest, a break, and was ready to go to the stable for the night. The master heard a voice coming from down the hill. An old, limping woman with her cane and a virgin she goat were coming. "Ah, no", said master to the champion, "we are about to have dinner and to go to bed!" The champion looked at him with eyes almost closed, because of fatigue and few dozen of coupling. His eyes were like "Oh Lord, spare me." The woman got closer and asked to get pregnant by the goat. I mean she asked for crossing between the champion and her virgin female goat.

"Please, I am coming from a far away village. This virgin is my only virtue and asset. Please, please get her pregnant. We need it."

"No." said the master, "my goat is tired, exhausted and short in sperm. He can't score no more. Come back tomorrow, you can stay here for the night if you want to. Early in the morning, he will do his best. I mean the champion will get your virgin goat pregnant, you'll be served the first."

"No, master. I have to go back to my husband, he is very old and he needs my attention."

"What are you talking about, you, yourself, are as old as my mother. How you can take care of another one?"

"This is our system and tradition. Wife is the servant of her man."

"I don't understand, you can come back tomorrow and . . ."

"We are very far away and please, I pay more than whatever you ask for," said the woman.

The man was muttering, talking about animal rights, looking at his goat, and said, "It is tough, it's already an overtime work and then a virgin, my Lord!"

"OK I will pay twice as much as your fee."

"Let me ask my goat." He went to his goat. He waked him up and pour some whiskey on his head and with an iron brush he rubbed few times his head up and down, front and back, back and forth. The iron brush was like an iron comb which was about to depeel the skin. In a second the goat was on his foot and ready to make love with the new comer.

When the coupling was done, the master got his money and the old lady paid for the crossing, and she was happy. She had a large smile on her face, and her eyebrows were up and down for many times. She left and the company went to sleep.

Early in the morning, the champion was out to eat some newspapers and the master got out to check the business and customers. He saw somebody down the hill, trying to walk up the hill, but no goat to get pregnant. The man came closer and the master saw an old man with a cane in his hand walking with difficulty and having a bandage around his head. He was injured at the front of his head. One could observe the color of blood underneath of the bandage. The man came closer and closer.

"Who is the goat master?" he asked.

"I am the one," replies the master.

"God damned, mother fucker, filthy race, son of a bitch! What did you teach to my wife?" and then he started to beat the master with his cane.

"What are you talking about?"

"You sent home an old lady with an iron brush. She brushed my front head like a crazy and asked me to make love with her. She did not stop until I had done it. Now I find you the responsible and guilty party and you have to be punished."

The master was about to defend himself and the goat. The very champion was looking at the scene of struggle and with a kick of his horns and head he gives an injury to the posterior side, upper thigh, and head of the old man. The old man was pushed and rolled toward the down hillside and left the scene miserably. He, of course, has injured the master, too, with his cane. The old man got home while limping and suffering from the ass injury.

"Who has done this to you?" asked the wife.

"The goat."

"The goat got your ass?"

"Yes."

"God have mercy."

"All your fault"

"Come one, we had a good day, yesterday. Plenty of achievements."

"Oh yeh?"

"Yes, and now you got it!"

"What did I get?"

"The goat blessing."

"If you call this a blessing?" and he went right away to bed.

"Yes, of course, goat and God are the same in terminology. When goat got domesticated by Sumerians, everything has changed. The civilization got started." The old lady had again a large smile and said to herself:—another good theory of mine. She took the iron brush and went to his man. The man was really like a dead person. She said to herself OK, we will have all options on the table.

The day pass and the day after, early in the morning the old woman took her cane and brush and went out toward the hilly side of the champion. "Anybody home?" she screamed from 100 feet from the stable. No answer. OK it seemed that the company was for a nap, before getting into another action. "Anybody home?" She knocked the door with her cane.

"What do you want?" asked the master while getting up.

"I want your goat."

"What are you talking about?"

"Your goat, stupid man, otherwise I will rub your head with this iron brush."

"Listen old lady, there are some rules and you have to play within the regulation frame."

Who makes these rules?"

"The international community."

"Who is the international community?"

"We are, me and my goat. He is like my arm. We are the new world order, but what do you want to do with my goat?"

"I want him to fuck me."

"What?"

"He has done it with my husband, that asshole person and I want him to do it with me."

"You asked for it!"

"Yes I am."

"You have to pay for it and pay me the damage."

"OK"

"Fucking Co. are very merciful, right? Especially for older generation and civilization.'

"Get me my Lord. Blessed be your people."

Amen.

PORTRAIT OF HOMER

In the University of Arts of the City of "Garden of San Marco", a bunch of students who are at the last and most important final exam, the "project", are supposed to make a portrait/sculpture which would represent Homer. The professor of the Visionary Arts, Mrs. Gardenier, is in her fifty's and is from a distinguished family, say an honorable tribe, making fortunes from art objects and antiques. She is from the same group of people who, as connoisseurs have the very last word about the value of a painting, sculpture, art object, etc. ; even if the "art object" is not an art at all and is a fake or valueless, useless, garbage or just a piece of shit. Of course these people select the best designs, fashions, designers, and their opinions are without doubt "the answer" to any question concerning Arts and Artists.

She is connected, into speculations and lobbying and promoting whoever is from or part of her surrounding people. In short she is of the "Art People" milieu. In her university class senior year there are thirteen students, belonging to three different groups. Group A has three students, all of them from the same "tribe" as the teacher, the same environment and the same social class under scholarship and grants provided by school, city, state and federal government. Group B with seven students all having the same aptitude and the same middle class families, are supported by parents, loans and their savings.

Group F has three students who have to work and support their parents while majoring in arts. They have a large amount of loans to pay back and they are, on average, older than the students of the previous groups. To respect the privacy act we will call them in connection with their group and will do this with letter and number as F1, F2, and F3.

F1 is a girl whose parent, her mom, is an emigrant from Latin America. In her art she is very sophisticated with colors and shapes and design, and very articulate, communicating even with her hands;

and though deep down, she is very good in heart and soul, she cannot show it. Her overweight body makes her unpopular, and her accent is a cause of distrust. In reaction, she is very rude and unwilling to open her mind to others. The rage of her rejection is often violent, making her impossible to work with.

F2 is a boy from India with a turban and unshaved beard, smelling like a spice shop, with tremendous ambitions. He is running after pennies, a gold digger and very tight fisted, meaning that he is very tough to get to spend for any thing at all. He is wearing the same clothes as in his freshman year even though in his neighborhood there are many thrift shops where he can buy old and secondhand things for almost nothing. But despite all these limitations his mind is not limited at all to his culture and narrow traditions. He has an ocean of ideas inside of his turban and brilliant logic and interpretation for his art works.

F3 is the oldest student of his class room. He is an emigrant, originally from Africa. He is not very dark but he is very happy with his curly hair. He is good with his hands and he knows what he is doing. He is slow, maybe because he has to work hard to earn his and his younger brother's living. He is a generous, lovable man but he has a terrifying voice.

As for A group, two girls and one boy, according to Mrs. Gardenier all of them are "Adorable", "Above others", and "Able" of any imaginable Art, By her judgment the quality of the work of the group A is, unmistakably, excellent and ready to explore the world of art and design.

As for B group there is nothing very particular to say, they are just followers, shadows of their shallow mind, trying to hang in there and to do what the leader is asking them to do. Good listeners to any advice made by the superior.

The final day for the completion of the design is tomorrow, declared Mrs. Gardenier. Since she was a busy professor, a very busy administrator and saleswoman and since she was, at the same time, the President of the University she had to organize her schedule in order to minimize the waste of time. For this reason she has decided to do the final project by groups of students and to examine and evaluate only three to four instead of thirteen. So she has given the "Portrait of Homer" to four groups as follows: Group A with three "magnificent" students, Group F with three "nasty" students and group B divided into two subgroups known as B1 and B2, B1 having four students and B2 having three students all of them known as the "Evangelical/ Angelical Students".Cnmwas

So Mrs. President, Professor Gardenier will have four projects to evaluate. Of course the evaluation is always done by a panel or jury

composed of several professors. Once again she announces by the overhead paging and loud speaker system the date for the project is tomorrow.

Group A has already finished its work. Group B has almost finished the job.

Group F has barely started and planned to work on it that night after their routine jobs. The time arrived and all three nasty students met at the library and exchanged ideas "How about a pyramid of dead bodies floating on an ocean of reddish water with a striking Hercules posing as Homer?" said F1.

"How about a Buddha holding the Iliad and Odyssey while entering the city of Troy?" said F2.

"Listen men, we are thirteen students. Let us take the book thirteen of the Iliad which is the assault on the ships." replied F3.

F2 said "Come on, let us stop the war and enjoy the peace. Let us have a dialogue between civilizations."

F3 said "OK I admit that I have my mind frame as a point of view. I am ready to collaborate on it, what-so-ever it is. Then let us combine the ideas and get the work done."

The night passed by and group F was on its project.

"The competition day is today." declares Mrs. Gardenier, while sitting behind her grandiose desk and asking the "jury" to join her.

The panel was ready and all students of the Art Major were in the auditorium.

"Please give applause to our jury members," said Mrs. Gardenier, "and then let us start to evaluate the student's projects or shall we say "competition" because they will enter the world of competition and smaller will be eaten by larger." She smiled and was very happy of with what she said. She shook her head a couple of times and from over her glasses gave an imposing look, arching an eyebrow and tilting her head toward the different groups of students for presentation of their projects.

Group A presented a picture of a soldier, fully equipped with all kinds of assault weapons, one of his hands showing a felt and the other one offering a can of Coke, while one of his feet is on the chest of injured baby on the ground.

Group B1 came up with a picture of a man holding the Iliad and Odyssey in one hand and a bow in the other.

Group B2 hands over a painting of a rhapsodist standing on a pile of books by Homer having a rifle or machine gun in his right hand and the left hand pointing at "you the people".

Group F came in with a smiling, loving Buddha, standing with his right foot on a stream of water. He has a dark skin and curly hair. His left foot is on top of a tomb of dismantled weapons. The source of the water is a light with the sign of all religions in a hug condition, making together something in that in cuneiform literature would read "Sumer".

Professor Gardenier and her colleagues of the university started to examine, interpret and grade all the competitor's work.

Everybody gave grade C for the two subgroups of Group B. All student of this group were so happy with this and cheerful. They were shouting and dancing and singing while professors were arguing about A and F Groups. An old professor who tried to give his idea about their work and give his observations and comments brought a widespread silence. "This work is a four dimensional picture, giving the impression of God death in a society of consumption and waste. It shows the Odyssey, "journey" toward light, peace, zarathustra, Persians and Sumerians, the pioneers of human civilization. You can feel and harvest the different time passing through the river and . . ."

"Come on, Mr. Nich. You're out of stream yourself." said Prof.

Gardenier. She then said "Won't you see the admirable work done by the

Group A"

"As the matter of fact, that is a promotion of consumption and . . ."

"No, this work of Group A represents a post-modern Art." replied a professor of Dr. Gardenier's entourage.

"What? Post-modern? Because of the Coke?" said Dr. Nich, the old professor.

"Yes, and because of the felt." said another jury member.

"Felt? What's felt have to do with Post-Modernism?" asked Dr. Nich.

"It means, if you don't want our production and our . . ."

"Yes," said Dr. Nich, while interrupting another jury member's sentence. "If you don't want our philosophy, then hell and the stone age era would be wanting you, I understand that, but . . ."

Dr Gardenier came to close the debate and said, "You're too old to picture the importance of this work and you're defending whatever has no meaning at all."

The critical moment of judgment is manifested and after the exchange of point of view Group A's work got an A+ and Group F's work was a failure.

Dr. Nich who was shocked by the unprofessional (or pure professionalism) act asked for retirement. At the board of trustee's meeting, the following day, not only his "resignation" was accepted but they charged him with felony. The three students of Group F have decided to work on a portrait of a "fiery and felted professor" as the "portrait of Homer" for the next semester.

STORY OF HER LIFE

My mom was sitting on her chair with her long scarf around her neck. She was looking at me from the corner of her eyes and watching me while I was writing.

"What are you doing? "she asks.

"I am writing mom."

"Are you sad?"

"Why"

"Because you're out of job and without . . ."

"Without what?"

"Nothing, you're here and helping me out for my day to day issues."

"I am here because I am living here, and I am like a dot."

"You mean like a dot com?"

"What are you talking about? What dot.com? What has a dot. com to do with me?"

"I mean, all these dots, without any dimension at all." I have all my dimensions." I said.

"Not me."

"You mean you're without any passion for anybody?"

"No, what I mean is, most of the writers I know don't have any dimension at all. They're like a dot." "You're a writer?" I said.

"You know . . ."

"Ah, you got that right, mom. Now I understand. You don't want me to write? Right?"

"You know, whoever is mad at somebody is writing. No message, no skill, no experience, no education, no goal, no ethics, no . . ."

"Mom, I have all the necessary experiences, education, and everything needed to be a writer."

"I know that honey, that's why I thought you're mad at somebody or sad over something or . . ."

"What do you want mom?" I said, while shaking my head and putting aside the pencil.

"I want you to write my story."

"OK." I showed my readiness while shaking my head. "Go on. I will write it down. Tell me your story."

She got off her chair and started to walk slowly. She stopped behind her chair and put on another scarf which was left there. I looked around and on another chair I saw a pile of scarves. She started to walk again, looked outside and went back to the scarves. She changed one of hers and I was waiting impatiently to see her done with her defilé. I said to her "Mom, make up your mind, I am waiting."

"Oh yeh. Write what I am going to tell you."

"OK mom."

"In the beginning it was dark; it was just a black-hole, with no singularity."

"Maaam!" I said, "What singularity? Do you know what that means at all?"

"I mean, no particularities, and everything was with God, the light, the word, money, prestige, power and glory." She looks up to the sky and continues. "And thanks to God some chosen people of his got everything, and . . ."

"You had a good husband too, right?"

She did not pay attention to my question and she was looking at her scarves.

'Mom?"

"Yes, No."

'Make up you mind, yes or no?"

"No, wrong, your dad was too soft. I needed a tough one, but he was soft."

"He was good though.» I reply.

"No I wanted him to fight for me, to kill other men for me, to be brave, and . . ."

"Mom, are you all right?"

"You'd better write it down before you forget."

"OK, OK. Go ahead."

"He did not like a pet at home, and I wanted very much to have a dog."

"How about a cat?"

"No, I don't like cats. Their saliva is not healing like dog's saliva which is very good for human health."

"What is your point mom?"

"You know, cats are cleaning themselves and their butt with their tongue, but dogs are cleaning other dog's butt, that's why their saliva is a healer."

I was thinking "Go and suck a dog's ass without any intermediate international company and its much better organic shit. Coming from factory to consumption." But I did not say it. It was gross. I left my mom to open her heart. She continued

"Your dad was soft and he liked fish as pets, because fishes are soft."

"So what?"

"He told me many times that if I want a dog I have to walk it, to clean it, to feed it myself. For your dad, fishes in a big fish tank, outside of the building, in the yard, do not harm anybody. He used to say: "Fish's saliva is good for the environment and I don't care about it.""

"I don't see your point mom."

"You better write down without interrupting."

"You see mom, you want to complain. Is it the story of your complaints that you want me to write down?"

"You're a woman, I mean you're a girl and you understand my feeling, don't you?"

"Of course I do."

"So your dad was too soft, he wanted to take care of his mom in this very house!"

"What was wrong with that?»

"Wrong? I'll tell you, first of all he did not want me to work; he wanted me to be free for him."

"What's wrong with that? Good for you if you did not have to go, every day, out of the house with all this traffic and crazy drivers and …"

"Listen my girl, you have the feelings of a woman. Women need to go out to work."

"What did you want to do?"

"I wanted to be a manager."

"Manager?"

"Yes." she said eagerly.

"Manager of what?"

"A manager. I don't care; that was your dad's responsibility to make me a manager."

"What kind of business?"

"Don't what what. He knew how to do it and he did not do it."

"You're not fair mom."

She waited for a little while and like a tiger which is hungry stood up and came toward me. I covered my head and she angrily, with her saliva in the air said "That was your dad's word."

"What word mom?" I said in a low tone.

"Fairness", that is your dad's word."

"Is it bad?"

"No, he wanted me to be fair with his mom."

"Why didn't you want my grandma here?"

"Because my mom was living with us."

"How lovely, they could have shared the same room. To talk together, and to have the company of each other."

"No, they could not get along together. They were always complaining that the other one wouldn't let her talk. Some time they were talking together at the same time. They were interfering and putting their nose into other's business. Most of the time they were going on like "lablablablab", because you couldn't follow them. Both of them were like tigers whose boundary and territory was not enforced by your dad. Your dad was too soft." She said this last sentence with a deep frown.

"You mean soft with his mom?"

"Yes, he couldn't say no to her. As a matter of fact he was watching them and laughing at them all the time. He used to say that "old people in the house are God's blessing", and above all his mom was Catholic and we're, I am at least, a Protestant. That was another main reason we couldn't get along."

"What was the difference?"

"She was all the time "Kyrie eleison".

"And this didn't please you I guess?"

"No. No. What is wrong with "God have mercy"? I don't like Latinos."

"You mean, everything should be in English, right?"

"Yes, I told you before, in the beginning there was word and word was with God and it was English."

"So, let it be. OK mom, what else was bothering you?"

She looked at me, without blinking for some time and then she shook her head a few times and then while collecting her saliva with the corner of her scarf, said

"I know that you can write it down yourself."

"What?" She had interrupted my chain of thinking where I have started the story of dad as a retired teacher. It was a good start, man, and now she wants me to continue by myself with her mountain of complaints she hides under her scarves, especially at the corner of her scarves.

"Don't say what," she replied. "Write! Put it in writing."

"OK mom, but don't complain if I write my own opinion about your biography."

"This is exactly that happens in the real world."

"What? How come?"

"Don't what. Write my autobiography like all writers who write autobiography of others."

"This is not autobiography anymore."

"That's my point, my dear."

"I have to have some hints."

"Ok. I'll give you some." she continues. "The black hole I was talking about was absorbing all lights and energies. It absorbed your dad before absorbing his mom."

"You mean, dad passed away before his mom did?"

"Yes and then her mom came to ask for some of your dad's assets."

"Some? How much some?"

"She was asking for one tenth of that."

"That was fair."

"No. Don't say that. Who decides what is fair and what's not?"

"Your consciousness, I guess."

"No. This matter will get to your lawyer and he or she decides."

"OK. If you think that is matter of his or her decision, let it be. Then what happened?"

"The justice was done and the court decided that one sixteenth is a good number."

"The grandma had other children? Yes?»

"No." "So?"

"So the court decided that after she passed away everything had to go back to your dad's children."

"What is exactly your complaint?"

"I wanted to be a manager. I wanted to be the one who gave her monthly allocation."

I shook my head and while looking at her from above my glasses said "I see your point."

"I wanted that something came out of the black-hole."

"That's it, mom, now I get it and I can come up with the story of your life."

She collects her saliva with the corner of her scarf and smiled at me and shook her head and said "That's my girl."

TEACHER OF "SEVEN HEAVEN" SCHOOL

I used to work in a pre-school institution for a few years. I mean, in a new institution where I was the first hired. This school was a private enterprise and the owner was a nice man called Nike. His wife was the accountant of the school and a manager called Nina was in charge of almost everything. She was a nice and knowledgeable person with a degree in early childhood teaching. She had a lot of good qualities. She was energetic and a hard working individual. She used to bribe teachers with her homemade cookies and pies. I don't know how she could manage to get enough time to accomplish all these fantastic activities. On top of that she was reviewing all lesson plans of all teachers. Yes. You've heard it right: "Lesson plan". Between us that was my invention.

Lesson plans for all babies, even for seven weeks old babies. I have to emphasis that we use to enroll kids from seven weeks of age up to 270 weeks old. Yes, the name of the school is coming from this sacred number. But, wait a minute another sacred number which is the foundation of heaven, is also used in this school. This number is twelve. Twelve is sacred from China to England. Of course the Sumerians or Babylonians were first to introduce that. Even though we have only ten fingers. They have maybe predicted that some babies will be born with a superdactyly condition. Oh yes, that is a good and reasonable explanation. So twelve was the number of infants in each class. Each class had three full time teachers and one halftime. This half time teacher use to work her first half time in another classroom. So I had almost three persons under my direction. Yes you got it. Right, I was the leader teacher of my classroom.

My class was for the new comers. Babies of seven weeks to thirty seven weeks. After this age the babies of my class graduated and went to the next class. Oh yes, with a graduation party. They have to be used to it. I mean we have to prepare our babies for consumption, for fun, for big words. Keep this in your mind. This is part of the plan. We have a lesson plan for our babies.

Don't ask me: "What is the plan for a baby of seven weeks of age?"

Don't tell me: "These babies can't get, yet, their bottle of milk in hand and they can't get their head strait."

I have good answers. We are taught to hide our head and watch their reactions.

Don't tell me: "They're very happy not seeing you with that fat belly of yours."

Of course, I have a very fat belly but I have my brain. Of course, I have a strange mid-south-west accent and sometime it's tough to understand me. By the way, it's not that hard. My first husband used to understand it very well. May be because he was an Asian immigrant with whole lots of patience. Poor guy. He left me because he couldn't get his visa. He did not leave me because of my accent or anything. The reason of his leaving, I told you, was a visa matter. That's what his friends told me later on.

Anyway. Now, I am the leader of our classroom. I told you that before, didn't I?

I am the leader for many good reasons. First of all, I am the best, and the heaviest one. Of course I am heavy but I meant mind wise I am the heaviest. Secondly I am the most experienced one. I've planned the lesson plan for our classroom. Before me there was no lesson plan for the infant room at all. Hey, don't tell me that I was the first one to get hired and before me, no Seven Heaven Preschool. Yes I know. What I meant is no lesson-plan at all anywhere. Parents know that without my lesson plans their kids would be good for nothing. Can you imagine a preschool infant room without a lesson plan? Of course babies can't talk but they very appreciate a good lesson plan.

For instance, hide your head for a moment and then get back in front of a baby, even a newborn one, and you will notice he or she will be happy to see you. Of course they can't talk or remember their early childhood but they will recall you and your hidden face, when they grow up. Another thing you can do is to make a soft ball with soft fabric and a hard ball like a golf ball and let babies to touch them, and to observe the differences. Oh yes. They can tell the differences if they can't talk. All girls would like the soft ball and boys are attracted by the golf ball.

They can't talk but you can observe in their eyes that they are learning and they are having fun.

Wait a minute; this experiment is easy to do. Have a brush and color it with paint and give it to them to paint. They will love to paint. I am not kidding. Listen. I am serious, ask yourself why a monkey can paint and why not your baby. Age doesn't matter. The painting of a master is not any better than the one done by a monkey or a baby. Of course your baby can't take the brush in hand but you can help.

What else? A hat, for example with fur and another one made of genuine wool. Leave it in front of babies. All baby girls will love the fur one and boys will love the wool one. Of course the wool must be a new comb, not a recycled one.

They can't walk or crawl to the hats, you would suggest, but you can see in their eyes. When you bring to a girl's eyes the fur one she is happier and the same thing with a boy and the wool hat. You see, you can now have a lesson plan for the newborns.

Another thing I have come up with is the idea is to show the grocery picture to them. As the matter of fact this is a good foundation for advertisement. You have to start as early as possible. That is what they have to do in order to be successful. I mean the advertisement companies have to follow it. My job is giving me the hint for this challenge. I am in this business for a long time and I am sure of what I am talking about. As the matter of fact that is why all parents give me gifts from time to time.

I've even proved with my observations that crawling of babies who go to other ones, is for touching their cloth to feel if its fur or a fake fur. You know, babies are smart explorers. Even later on if they bite each other it's because they want to know how soft the other is one's flesh and skin. They hate goose bump skin.

Listen to this, one day I put the babies address and picture on an envelope and I stuck it on the wall in front of their crib. Then what? Believe it or no they loved it. They thought they had received a letter from themselves. That was fun for them. After that, pretty soon they will get ready to see their image in the computer monitor. That's for sure! This is how we predict the future. I am sorry that I couldn't do it with my own kid. I mean, to do the very same experiences. That is why my kid is not good with the computer. That is a shame right. You have to have a lesson plan. A good one.

Let them for example to touch the toothbrush. At an age of say six months, they know it's for cleaning the teeth and they bring it right away to their moth. They don't have teeth but they know if they had the brush would be the tool to clean. They are smart this new generation of nanotechnology babies. Does it mean they are going to get smaller in size? I don't know, and I don't care, it's better for me if they're smaller. They don't give me a bad back because of their weight,

Oh yea. Another hint. Put some dentifrice on top of a tooth brush and give it to a baby. He or she will tell you which bran is the best by accepting it or repulsing it. Sometime they don't want to get it because the dentifrice is not good. It's that simple.

Ah, you know I have hundred of observations good enough to write a book. After all I am a leader in my classroom. I have to acknowledge this fact that I know what I am talking about. Ironically, one day, our company has decided to hire another teacher because one of mine left the school. I don't know why teachers don't stay longtime in my classroom. May be they know with all my knowledge and experience they don't have smallest chance to get promoted to a higher level. Anyway, the new teacher was coming from another institution of a small city. She got hired and get started in my classroom.

I couldn't get her name. She was like a grandma and she was like she is pretty sure of her experience and knowledge about early childhood. She had a masters degree in I don't know what field and she was awarded the best teacher of the year, I don't know how and for what reason. Her name was who cares. I did not like her manner and attitude. She got in and she said "Hello, nice to see you guys and delighted to be part of this family of caregivers." What arrogance. Here we don't say Hello, it's not necessary and we avoid useless conversations.

And she was mediocre in English. She was slow and her accent was terrible. I don't like people with heavy and strange accent.

She had a sort of smile on her face and she was inviting parents for chat and conversation about their kids. I don't like that. We don't do that here. Her angelic face and her smiles and "Hello, good mornings, goodbye . . ." who cares? It's not good for babies. What we need is a lesson plan.

The very same day she got hired I told to my coworker Nancy, I said: "Who cares about your F. name? She's got to get to work."

Nancy said: "Her name is Nour and she said it means "light"."

"Oh yea. She is not even a candle. Light! My ass."

Nancy said: "Get the poopy out of your lips."

I thought because of my language and vocabulary she said that but she shouted again, "The poopy, you have a diaper in hand for longtime and the poop is all around your face because you get excited while insulting that other one."

"Kiss my ass, "I said and went to a mirror. As the matter of fact I had few touches of poop on my face. That is how I am working. I put my soul into my head. Then I return to the "grandma" and I said: "Get started. You have four babies but since you just got started, take care of one of mine and one of Nancy's."

She did not say a word and got started. Nancy said: "She seems to know her job" "Shut up, "I said.

"Mr. Nike said that Nour is a laureate national price for best teacher and she knows two foreign languages."

"What is important is English and she is slow and secondly the most important thing is the lesson plan. I know she was hired to replace me and I don't want to listen to these F. garbage." I said to Nancy: "Nancy, can you see her, I mean the "grandma-without-any-lesson-plan" to be able to replace me?"

"But"

"No but. You know that I don't make any mistake with my judgments" I said.

"You have made a wrong judgment about your boy friend, "she replied, "and you thought he is going to marry you in a couple of months. Two years passed and still he is not decided."

"It's not true, "I said. "He wants me to go for a volume reduction of stomach by surgery and he says that I am eating too much. But you know it's not true. I have a big belly because that is my genes."

"What genes?" she said.

"Shut up Nancy, let us get back to her. Then I went to the "grandma" and I said,

"What is you lesson plan?"

"What?" replies the new teacher.

"What what? You got to have a lesson plan for new born babies.' I said.

"Oh yes, as the matter of fact I have one," she said. "My plan is to give them the best of love I have had and I had for my own children. I am going to give them my soul and I will sing for them, I will nourish them. I will satisfy their needs, I will give them a secure surrounding. I will clean their environment from any pollution. I will replace their parents while they are at work. They need to know the benefits of good parents. They need to know how to appreciate their sacrifice. In their eyes I see the Heaven and the Seven Heaven. I put my vision and my heart, as Jean Piaget said."

"Hey. Stop it. Seven Heaven is the name of this school and don't use it without their permission. It's gone be costly for you," I said. And this was a good start.

Nancy came to me and pushed me in a corner and said" "I don't like her, she has a big mouth, don't waste your time and let us destroy her as soon as possible. In a country where patent is so important she is using their name for her vision. Isn't it funny?"

"Yea We're gone get the F. bitch" "The shit", Nancy said.

"What?"

"Once again you have poop on your face," she said.

"Shit. I am embodied by poops." I said, and I went to the bathroom to clean my face and when I got back my boy friend was there and it was time to leave.

"I am going to leave," I said." We'll get in touch and I'll be working on the subject with my boyfriend"

"Ok. I'll see you. "said Nancy.

And without saying a word to that bitch I left the school.

During our trip to home, via a fast-food restaurant, I discussed the matter with my boy friend who was a good expert of video-monitoring, and he came up with a good, an excellent idea. As soon as tomorrow we will put two video cameras in the room to register our activities without showing the grandma at all. Even when she is working with her assigned babies the video will show us to work on them. But if she takes a sit and a rest the video will register her. After a week or so when we are about to have a meeting with parents we will talk about our new lesson plan and will show the videos. That was an excellent idea.

You know that the grandma starts to work at 10:00AM and finishes at 6:30PM and so, we had enough time to install our video. When she got to work everything was settled and she did not notice anything. This kind of video game is good. It is good for spying and monitoring and everything.

Meanwhile, no talk with the bitch even though she was nice! So called "nice". She was always, "Hello, good morning, God Bless . . ." This kind of F, useless vocabulary. One week passed and we had the open house meeting with parents.

What a day! You can't believe it. I came up with a new "Lesson Plan" and they loved it. The only person who objected was the grandma. Good for me. You know if God wants to destroy someone, we have to follow him.

You want to know about the lesson plan? Don't you? OK. I'll talk about it. But you have to imagine the surrounding environment. Parents were there. The Director gave a lecture. He introduced the teachers and talked about Nour. He said about her experiences and

I was laughing inside of me and looked at Nancy. With my regards I said' OK. I'll F. you later on."

The Director, then gave the podium to the manager. She gave some information about the new rules and I was busy with my plan; and my lesson plan.

Finally she asked me to go to the podium, as the most experienced teacher.

I went to there. I said: Get ready with my lesson plan and my videos." All parents get excited.

My lesson plan for new born classroom is, you know, I mean, you understand what I mean. I was a bit nervous. I said we will have the main colors. Every week a new color for the room and we will repeat the name of the color all the time.

Parents were silent and curious. I said, for instance the first day the room will be blue and each time we get to the room or to each infant we will say" Blue." Or you want a "blue"?, what we mean is you want your bottle? Or you did "blue". (pope). You xxx blue. This would be the name of the day and of the week. Another thing. All day long we don't use our name we will say for example, blue come and clean that blue. The next week the room color will be red. And so on.

Parents were looking at me like they're looking at a goddess . . . Nothing but admiration. One of them said: "Don't you thing they are too young for your experience?"

"Not at all. They need to know that. This is good for fashion industry to see what kind of color is preferred by this new generation." I said.

"Are you sure?" another mom said. "Don't you think it's gone scare out babies?"

People return their face to the grandma. She was like doubting the fact. Fortunately, the Director came to my rescue and said: "Why don't you want to show your video?"

"OK, "I said. And my boy friend came to my rescue here. And show started. The real show. No censorship in this country. We are proud to be vigilant and in the forefront of leadership roles and programs. Watch this. The videos were excellent. Nothing but true. You've better believe it; that was showing friends and foes. It was a good turmoil for the bitch. I said "Don't forget it: We are children of hurricane," The mates of the universe.

THE DADDY'S EARS

From a short trip to France, I was coming back home. I went to Paris to see a friend of mine who was sick and needed my help and advice. What way I could have been helpful and wise? That was a good question. Especially the fact that I was between jobs and my mind and my wallet were as empty as my galaxy and cosmos.

He, as thoughtful he is, sent me a return plane ticket in order to eliminate all excuses. While in Paris, we managed to review his "will" and we accepted I would look over the kids if he has passed away. He has only one boy and he calls him the daddy's ears. This analogy was strange to me. I have seen many different names, like: honey, sherry, sweety, Dad's heart, love, kiss, cabbage, pumpkins, bonbon, dove, canary, virtue and so on, but never "ears of Daddy". What do you expect? Everybody has his or her own taste,

One day we were walking in the Jardin de Luxembourg. It was a calm day with beautiful weather. The horizon was so clear when we went down to the river front, a la the Seine and as we walked I asked and asked questions, tons of them. Why he has changed his name? Why he has remarried?

He replied, "My second wife did not like my name and I have changed it."

"Why "Paul" and not another thing."

"Because Paul is the bridge."

I was stupefied. I said, "You're sure?" "Yes I am.

"You mean you will say like the Golden Paul? Or Brocklin Paul? And don't you think your name is your identity?"

"No, many people immigrating to another country change their names. It has nothing to do with the identity. My identity is my inner substance and culture. On the other hand, did I choose my name in the first place or did somebody do it for me?"

"What is culture? First of all give me a definition for that."

"Don't get me in a conversation where you will talk non-stop."

"No, no, no, it's not true, I am a good listener."

"You used to be . . . you used to have such a beautiful ears."

"What a compliment!"

Then we got involved in talking about culture and traditions and peoples, who for their own good, to preserve their own culture, traditions and heritage are ready to destroy other people's culture, traditions and heritages. Then I sadly left him to come back home. I took the subway. When the "metro" stopped at a station some people got out of the train and some got in.

A young man got the seat in front of me. He had a pair of beautiful ears, so beautiful that I started to talk with him. He had a book of J. Foucault in hand and I asked him about his college and the system of education, grading and majoring, elective and minor courses. He was brief and certain in the answers but he was listening more than talking.

We arrived at the Charles de Gaul Airport and we said goodbye to each other.

Four hours later I was on my way to come back home, to Washington D.C. In the plane I was alone and I had a seat next to the window. I had closed the window shade for some time to get a nap. But all of a sudden I saw my ears. I had bigger ears than before, Oh my God!. And my ears were covered with hairs. I did not like it at all.

I remembered when I started to go out with my first girlfriend, who became my wife, she used to tell me that I had beautiful ears. I was so happy with my ears that I wanted to show them off at each moment. I wanted to have them big and exposed. Instead my nose was big so big that it was announcing my entrance to any place before I came in. Why God did not want to help me out in this matter? For him that was easy, to change the ear volumes, to replace their places, which would have been ears size replaced by nose size. Anyway, there is no use of complaint now with my zenith of beauty covered with hairs.

I got home and right away I tried with my electric shaver to get rid of the hairs. It did not work. I tried my razor blade. That was cruel. I cut all over different places of my beautiful piece of art.

I asked my wife to use the tweezers. She was now the cruel one. She did it even when I was sleeping and in the middle of the night.

I asked her to stop it and do it with cold wax and then warm wax and hot wax. Nothing good out of it.

Finely I went to my dermatologist who as the matter of fact is my nephew.

He looked at them and said "Uncle, nothing wrong with your ears, but as for your hearing, you need a device."

"Thank you dear, you're a Dad's ear, and uncle's . . ."

"What?"

"Nothing, what I mean is you're our pride."

"Ah, how nice! You're my best uncle."

"You have only one, and I am the best between one contestant. Thanks to God I am not the second."

We laughed and made appointment for the next dermatological ear visit!!!"

THE SALE OF A HOUSE

Mr. Al wanted to sell his house and move to another spot. He retired and his house was too expensive for a retired person living on a Social Security pension. At the same time, after thirty years of work for the same institution and thirty years of living in the same house and the same neighborhood he was so accustomed to his routine that it pained his heart to separate from them. But what do you expect; his wife was the boss and had had enough of the same pictures. Especially for the fact that some of the old next door friends had passed away and new faces came in and the texture of the neighborhood had changed. Their house was one of the fifty houses built in an old farm now very close to the train station and close to the shopping street and every other place of socialization for Mr. and Mrs. Al. Even their church was in walking distance. The hospital, the doctors, the library, banks, you name it, were all in a radius of just one mile. Everything was there.

Of course, too many conveniences are not conveniences. This is the argument of a new generation. They aren't happy with what they have. They need problems. It's like an old saying: "A man was squeezing his own testicles and screeching with pain. "Why are you doing this?" asked his friend. "Because when I don't do it, it is heavenly nice." So, people would like to squeeze their own testicles. May be this is the human nature. By this argument what is a woman squeezing?

Anyway, Mr. Al asked an old friend to help him with the sale of the house. His friend was a very talented person. A realtor who was thirty years in the business, called Ms. Meehan, got involved in his project right away. She came and asked them to get rid of all old furniture and things which were part of Mr. Al's identity. But, since she was their realtor and their consultant, the Als had nothing to say.

In one week the house was ready to go to market. The floor was sanded to hard wood, the painting renewed, the windows changed.

The appliances got replaced; something like twenty thousand had been spent for the house, and finally the wall between the kitchen and the living room was torn out. A brand new house was about to go to the market. Ms. Meehan's daughter helped to put a "House for Sale" sign at the corner of the street. At once people came to visit the house. The market was so hot that all houses got sold before getting listed, and a competition for the price would increase the price as much as twenty percent of the listing price.

Knowing this Ms. Meehan suggested "Let us go for three hundred thousand dollars for the listing and people will compete and the house will be sold for at least three hundred and sixty thousand."

"OK" said Mr. Al, "We have another fridge, and an old chandelier, curtains, a showcase, an old piano and other stuff that will come with the house."

"We will have all these in the listing." replied Ms. Meehan, "and may be another five to ten thousand would be added to the price." said Ms. Meehan.

"Mr. Al was speechless, quiet and a little sad while witnessing his past going out the door.

Ms. Meehan went home and the Als went out for dinner because Ms. Meehan asked them not to cook anymore in order to have everything as clean as brand new. They came back from the restaurant and Ms. Meehan called right away and said "I want to see you, I have an offer."

"Come on, that is good news."

Ms. Meehan came back and she sat down. It was like she is suffering from shortness of breath.

"Are you all right?" asked Mrs. Al.

"Yes, Yes. I was walking fast and I am very busy."

"My daughter wants your house and since I am representing the buyer and the seller at the same time, I will have only 3% of commission fee and so it will be additional money in your pocket."

"What good news. We are happy to see the house going to a person we know. If you enjoy it we will be glad and we will welcome the offer." said Mr. Al.

Ms. Meehan shook their hands and said "The official papers will be handed to you tomorrow." And she left.

Mr. and Mrs. Al were looking at three hundred sixty thousand dollars and were elated to call friends and family and asked another friend in the countryside for a house which would be cheaper but bigger. The surplus would be for additional retirement savings.

"The next day, as promised, Ms. Meehan handed them an envelope of the realty company with the offer inside. She got Al's signature for getting the house out of the market and the listing right off, even though the house has never even gotten listed and never got on the market. Then she left immediately, giving the excuse of work. And then Mrs. Al opened the envelope and saw the official offer with sealed signatures and every necessary document included, asking Al to sign and to finalize the transaction. But there was a surprise; the offered price was only three hundred thousand dollars!

Mr. and Mrs. Al were like cats put in cold water. Mr. Al was so angry that he started to yell insults and scream and to pace around. That night they could not sleep. Ms. Meehan has done her masterpiece, and slept like a happy bear.

The next morning they asked Ms. Meehan about the offer and she came over and gave a list of excuses while presenting herself as full of good will and the best intention and reaffirming that the price was very good and the only three percent commission would be so advantageous.

"You bought this house for one hundred thousand and now you will sell it for three times as much as you bought it for." said Ms. Meehan.

"Yes, but that was thirty years ago," said Mr. Al "and I know that the worth of the house is four or five times more than thirty years ago."

"The last house sold, in your area, for two hundred and fifty thousand and this affects your house's price."

"That was the price of ten years ago. Since then nobody has sold their house in our neighborhood."

"This is how we price a house."

"Let us forget your offer and get the house listed, "said Mrs. Al.

"OK but don't forget that you have signed the form of "sole realtor" and I will be yours for the next six months. Even if you sell your house I will get my commission."

Mr. Al said "We don't want to sell the house and we will forget about our silly decision."

"You have an engagement and you have to pay my daughter's damage."

"We will go to the court." said Mrs. Al.

Ms. Meehan was so angry that she was shaking and then crying and then said "Mr. Al, you have never been happy with me, you never smile, and you act always like an enemy." She was crying with her eyes full of tears.

"If I donate my house to your daughter, then you will be happy? What do you want me to smile and to be happy about? I know why you are crying. You are in a wrong position which is a conflict of interest. From one side your daughter and from the other side your long real estate career and this struggle will give you a split personality. Of course, the mom aspect is more obvious and apparent than the friendship one, too."

"God knows that in this transaction I have given you all the benefits of my friendship."

"Don't bring God into this matter." said Mrs. Al.

"Let us have dinner together and forget about business."said Mr. Al.

"No, I have to go. My daughter is expecting me. I will call you tomorrow for your decision." "OK." said Al's wife.

She left and the old husband and wife were so amazed by the kind of persons who get around people when there seems to be the potential to get some money. Then they called the friends and relatives who knew laws and regulations. All of them advised unanimously; go to court.

"Listen my love; if we go to court we might get her but how about our nerves and souls. What of our peace of mind and our state of health? Let us do it and accept the offer. This is what God has brought to us." said Mr. Al.

"Ok Let us do it. And we will leave it to the hand of God." replied Mrs. Al.

"If he has hands."

"Don't be silly."

"OK. OK. Sorry."

They called and asked Ms. Meehan to go ahead. "OK, I will send an inspector for the inspection."

"We agreed that the house will be sold as is. "said Mr. Al.

"Yes but the mortgage company of my daughter requires this and she will pay for it."

"OK"

"Please don't be at home tomorrow afternoon between two to five PM."

"OK"

The next day afternoon Mr. Al came home to rest in the patio while sitting and reading. It was about 4 PM and the Meehans and their inspector were there.

The inspector left open or unscrewed whatever he took off and unscrewed from the watering hose, to the faucet, to the AC and washing machine and dishwasher.

"Why is the facet open and everything misplaced?" "This is my way of working." said the inspector.

"And then what?"

"Then nothing, you will put it back to the initial place." "You will pay me for it?" said Mr. Al.

"No. This is your obligation."

"What a stupid regulation."

"You've better watch what you're saying." "Leave it to me, Mr. Al" said Ms. Meehan.

Mr. Al went back to the patio and got to his reading but his blood pressure was so high that he could not understand what he was reading. A few minutes later his wife came back home from work and they went out for dinner.

After they came back from dinner Ms. Meehan came to hand over another letter and complain about Mr. Al's behavior regarding the inspector's work. Once again Mr. Al's blood pressure went up and up to a point that he got a heart pain and shortness of breath, when he saw that Ms. Meehan's inspector was asking a thousand dollars to fix whatever things are damaged in the house. Even though these things were donated by Al's family and they were not part of the house. Ms. Meehan wanted them in good shape, despite accepting to buy the house as is.

"Don't do business with friends and family, stupid man." said Mr. Al. to himself. The closing date was at three PM in two days at the real estate company and with now wide opened eyes the Als went. Now Ms. Meehan was asking for six percent commission. Fortunately the Als family had the appropriate letter including that the commission was fixed at three percent but still she was not happy and asking for more discount, while waiting for her daughter to arrive for the necessay signatures.

Her daughter came in with a bunch of roses in one hand and a bottle of champagne in the other. As she came in she said "Mom, I went to visit the house before signing the document. Everything is in the best condition and look, the roses and the champagne were left in the fridge for us with Mr. and

Mrs. Al's letters of welcoming."

"Oh yeh?"

"Yes."

"Something must be wrong; otherwise that kind of kindness is not normal these days."

"Are you sure?"

"Yes. Let us go and check the house. We need our inspector." They left in a hurry.

Al's family had already signed the documents and was waiting to get their check.

The broker who was from the mortgage company was nice enough to hand over the check with no problem and said "Don't worry. I will take care of the rest."

"God bless you and thank you very much. "said Mrs. Al. Mr. Al was so exhausted he was like a deaf-mute and also very hungry.

They left the city of civilized people and went to a small village far away from the town. A month later you could have heard that a strong hurricane had demolished their old part of the city and Ms. Meehan's home was gone with the wind and she went back to a mediocre neighborhood.

Location. Location. Location.

THE SECRET OF MY UNCLES

There are three of them. All the same, self-centered, and very much like my grandma. She used to have a good influence on them. That is why they're living in the same neighborhood in order to come to visit my grandma almost every day or every other day. The youngest was a bit more volatile. He tried to disobey the rules from time to time and obviously he was the subject of complaints and arguments. We used to live with the grandma, because my dad passed away at a young age and my mom, obviously, as a single mom and still young and attractive was offered a room for the rest of her life, in their house, with food and pocket money. We were four kids, one boy and three girls, and we did not know by who and how this service was provided to us because the grandpa was not a full-time employee and he used to work for the uncle's company. Let us say that the day to day readiness of food was a miracle and according to grandma, the miracle happened, only, for her family, and for her tribe of twelve branches. Make no mistake, this tribe of grandparents and six children and four grandchildren was as sacred as any twelve in the cosmos, like the twelve signs of the zodiac, and the twelve months of a year of the Babylonians, twelve apostles, twelve sons of Isaac, twelve Imams of the Shi'a branch of Islam etc . . . The only difference was that these in the history of religions were all male and here in my grandma's mythology it was seven males and five females. My grandma was even more proud of this combination of the seven heavens and five elements of daily life. You got it right, five elements including the earth, wind, fire, water, and ether, the influence of eastern mythology and philosophy on her character. Of course the reason was the respect for elders and dead ancestors of the family in the eastern civilization.

Back to my uncles. The oldest was one and a half year older than the second one. The second one was two and a half years older than the third one. Then the girls showed up. The oldest one was three and a half years younger than the youngest boy and four and a half years older than the second daughter who was five and a half years older than the last daughter. I guess, in between, some abortion or miscarriage had taken place but the existing combination was fabulous and a long period of time, almost 18 years, elapsed between the first and the last child.

This meant practically two sets of birthdays for all the family. The grandpa's birthday closed one set and grandma's birthday the other set. Grandma was amazed by this coincidence and would call it again and again as a miracle. While she was talking about it enthusiastically, grandpa would be looking at her and then used to turn back his eyes to his sons, one by one, while puffing at his almost dead pipe. Grandma would be shaking her head and crossing her heart and passing the message to her daughters. The girls were looking at each other and shaking their head in their turn.

But again, back to my uncles. Sorry, but wouldn't you agree that all their understanding and behavior was the impact of their previous environment? Of course yes.

My oldest uncle was more handsome than the others. He was the president of a small firm of general construction company, specializing in roofing. They used to make and repair different kind of roofs for old or new buildings and mostly old ones. The other members of the company were my two other uncles and of course my grandpa. Each of them had a title, like General Manager, CEO, and so on. Oh, I almost forgot the secretary and the janitor, who used to make coffee and tea for the "institution' and customers.

The janitor was an old immigrant man, older than my Grand Pa with a very horny temperament, by that I mean he wanted women. Most of the secretaries were escaping the "institution", after few months on the job, because of his sexual harassment. He was very direct kind of guy, as we learned later in our "research"! He used an approach to those secretaries like "You sleep with me?".

My grand pa was always for firing him, but my uncles loved him and were sympathetic to him because he was a poor and lonely man, with nobody in his surrounding milieu.

I don't know why the janitor kept acting like this. May be he had some success in the past. But, still, it was absurd. He had rather unpleasant features, with a long head like a horse. His lips were odd and uneven. His eyes were like bulging out, pop-eyed, with no eyebrows and he had plenty of white mustache. His lower part of the body, I am not entitled to describe, because I've never seen it, it was probably a better shape.

My older uncle, who we used to call "the Senior", was always joking about him and together with my grandpa and "the Medium", the second uncle, and "the Junior", the youngest uncle were all laughing and gossiping over him. They used to call him: "Mr. Ynroh" pronounced like "inrow". Since Ynroh has uneven lips, and was speaking from the left corner of the mouth, he could not pronounce some words correctly. And the Senior used to tease him by asking him to say "Ptolemy pooped on a poor pet." And so with Ynroh it was like he was blowing in a trumpet when the world "p" was to be pronounced. He would be blowing and pumping from the left side of the mouth and some words would be coming out and again he would be pumping and blowing and my uncles would be laughing and laughing hard. The Senior would have tears in his eyes and my grandpa's chest would be heaving up and down and he would be coughing and laughing at the same time.

The Medium was a rather course person and he wanted to know how Ynroh's manhood is built. He once asked him whether he can make love with his own ass. Ynroh replied "What do you mean?"

My uncle replied "Is your pépé long enough to reach your ass?"

The answer was "Yes, yes, yes!" Obviously he wanted to impress the secretary.

Then, the junior said "You can poop on your own pépé!" Everybody laughed and meanwhile the secretary was upset and getting red up to her ears.

The junior was "Hey Ynroh, your pépé has effect even with people's ears!"

My grandpa used to asked them not to go too far with joking, especially when a lady is present in the office area. But Mr. Ynroh was never embarrassed by my uncles. He loved it. He always encouraged the conversation to that level in order to get more familiar with secretaries and at some point in order to testify to his self-judged large pépé. The secret of Mr. Ynroh was always confined to the office and was only for the working environment.

At home, the boys were sometime laughing to themselves and my grandpa would look at them with an unhappy expression and shake his head a few of times from right to left and vice versa to show his frustration and dissatisfaction. But then his sons were encouraged to laugh more. My youngest uncle would say to us kids "If you're not good boys, then Ynroh will get you". With this phrase my grandpa would get more upset and with his finger pointing at them, one by one, would shake his head up and down and with his eyes staring hard would be threatening them without saying a word.

The Senior was: Oh, oh! Then there would be a moment of silence and the subject would get changed. The Junior would look at grand-ma and with a tiny smile, would look at each of the others while moving his eyebrows. The others would all be again laughing like crazy.

The rest of us, mom's kids, didn't understand a thing about their signs and just got more curious. Sometimes, we were about to call them "moron" or "crazy", or "loonies". We would look at each other in order to mock them and then laugh loudly. My mom and my grandma would say 'What?" My grandpa would then say, "What, "What"?" and everybody would be laughing, my uncles and my mom and grandma and grandpa finally

One day after all these back and forth conversations, the Senior looked at the Junior and then turned his eyes to the Medium while he was bending to pick up his toothpick from the floor. His pants were getting loose and the starting groove of his butt was exposed. Then the Junior moved his eyebrows up and down and then he moved his head with a blink in one eye. The Senior exploded with laughter and the Medium turned his head back toward them and pointed his finger toward them and said "I'll asked the Lord Ynroh to get you, if you don't stop it." They laughed and again we did not understand it. Then he repeated the same remark while looking at the Senior and giving him the sign. Finally the Senior and the Medium looked at the Junior without saying anything and after another deep look at him they exploded with laughter and said" Oh Lord Yuroh." My grandpa finally smiled while he was reading his Holy Book and we did not know what was their secret.

After we had grown older we got to know the reason for their laughter by accident. As a matter of fact the accident was the funeral of Mr. Ynroh. The same day that we all were at the funeral. The viewing, what can I say, he was an ugly man but in peaceful rest. At last in piece with his pépé. We were sitting while my grandpa was about to give a short talk. He had barely started and my uncles were looking at each other, and my grandpa noticed their intention and brought an angry expression to his face. With a deep and piercing glare he gets them to calm down. Then my grandpa started his speech and said "Mr. Ynroh, peace of the Lord upon his soul, was an honest man,", At this point the Senior looked at the others and moved his eyebrows up and down while looking at the grand-pa and shaking his head as if to say "What a yami!". The other uncles were so ready for an explosion. At the very same time grandpa was at the end of his talk and was saying "He was a hero to my sons. May Peace of the Lord be on him," but instead of saying "be" he said "pe" and my uncles laughter exploded and then everybody laughed. My grandpa just went on "You know, Mr. Ynroh had a hard time to pronounce "p" and that is maybe why I said "pe" instead of "be". He finished his talk and turned his head toward the corpse of Ynroh and smiled. My uncles laughed again. Later in the day after the dinner, the grandpa told a brief history of the office of roof construction and some of my uncle's reasons for laughing.

THUS SPOKE MINESTRONE

"Our last subject is Post-modernism and after that we will have the finals." Thus spoke the Professor of Philosophy at the College of Philosophy of the University of New World.

"As you know," she continues, "our philosophy is analytic and philosophy in Europe and especially in France it's rather synthetic. As far as Post modernism is concerned we are neither analytic nor synthetic. In other words the definition of this philosophy is like minestrone. Thick vegetable soup."

"Good definition." said one of the students.

"I am hungry." said another one.

"What is the relationship between soup and philosophy?" asked another one.

"Wait a minute and you will understand." said the professor. She continued to make minestrone. "The chef has whatever is left over from the prior days. For example in a large pot he or she will put peas and beans, rice, carrots, mushrooms, celery, and whatever they can't use today. If no peas are left from yesterday they will change the recipe and finally he or she will add tomato soup of yesterday or leftover ketchup, or days old spaghetti sauce and that is why the dominant taste of the soup is tomato sauce. You can pour it on your rice and it will be a Chinese special or you can have a specialty of the house and you will call it specialité de la casa, if you add some cheese."

"Professor, are you giving a cooking lecture?" asked one of the girls in the class.

"No. I will be on the track. Please wait."

"Don't you use salt in your recipe?" asked another girl.

"She has a high blood pressure, Professor." said a boy and everybody laughed.

"She will give another lecture for dress making and embroidery." a boy said.

Everybody laughed at him.

"As a matter of fact I will." she replied, "once I get to the Postmodernism and art."

"O Lord have mercy." all students reply.

"OK, enough is enough. That was a break and let us get back to work." she said and continued, "So you will see that the ingredients of the soup will change according to our reserve in leftovers but still the taste is the same. Everybody in the kitchen can do it, you don't need any special talent for that sauce. You're putting into the pot whatever you have in your environment. Your customer can't say "Yesterday your minestrone had celery and mushroom but today it has rice and eggplant in it.""

"Can we make a pizza out of that to be delivered here?" asked a boy and everybody laughed.

"Of course and shut up." said the professor and continued again "If you ask a philosopher to give a definition for Post-modernism he or she will tell you that the definition is depending upon the field. In literature or poetry it's like the minestrone with no trace of any ingredients at all. Since they're smashed and the rest is a thick amalgam of everything which resembles nothing. It has the color and the taste of the market."

"You mean like rap music's lyrics?" asked one of the students.

"No, in rap music lyrics, you have a rhythm, you have a harmony and musical sentences. Here as I told you, you take everything, you smash it, crush it, and spit it."

"Is it like a vomit?" ask another one.

"Yuck" said all other students.

"Sort of." said the professor. "I told you, this is a nutrition class. I am going out for coffee and smoke a cigarette." The professor agreed to give a five minute break. When five minutes passed all students got back to the class room.

"I gave you the definition of Post-modernism in literature and now for in the arts. It has to be shocking and terrifying or it has to put you in a corner where you're checkmated. It has to have no relation whatsoever with art. I'll give you an example. You put your butt on the copier and take a copy and that is it. You frame it and you sell it."

"No color?" asked one student.

"Blue." said the professor.

"Why blue?" asked the same student.

"Because the butt is a sad area."

"Not mine!" replied the same student.

"She is constipated, that's why she is saying that it's a sad area," said another student. Everybody laughed.

"The color has no meaning. I told you, remember the pot of minestrone." replies the professor. "As long as you shock people that will do it."

"Bigger butt will shock more." said one of the girls.

"Like yours." said another one. Everybody laughed some more.

"In architecture," said the professor, "you mix the old style with new technology but no significant design is the best. You will see, at the centre of your creation a statue of Venus holding a Coke in hand and the Coke is like pouring into a spring and fountain below it, and the laser light will do the rest. You see you mix them up and you shock people and there is no meaning but consumption, marketing and illusion. You have to persuade people that they are happy and shocked as why they don't have the new merchandise. The architecture brings to question whatever is charming, classic, useful and long lasting."

"Finally we get to philosophy and psychology." says the professor.

"Easy when you don't understand anything." said one student, "then you're in good luck."

"No, " replied the professor, "in philosophy, each philosopher has his or her own definition and principle but for sure there is no place for God. God is dead. Instead there is a force, the internal force of consumption. In mind, you have to prepare people for consumption, pollution and wasting and recycling."

"Recycling? How come?" asked a student.

"Recycling at the old weapons in some area of the world by creating a war and replacing it by the new generations of more sophisticated ones."

"I don't see the pot of minestrone here." said a girl.

"Soup of bullet and bombs." replies another one.

"No, the soup is the mixture of all previous philosophy in the pot with the task of globalization of the economy." replied the professor.

"You don't put cheeses?" asked a girl.

"You do, as a matter of fact, and you add some spices which are human rights. You define it as you're pleased. You deconstruct what was built by others you have the materials and you sell it one by one as plurality. This is like from your pot you sell the ingredients. Of course they are squashed and you know it but poor people don't. They buy it. They buy the squashed peas, beans . . . So they are new stuffs in hand.

In the area of psychology you do the same thing. The old imagination triangle of mother, dad, and child is not valid anymore. There is a pot of minestrone. The child is exposed to consumption, no father, instead there is the "street" the effect of the street like kids born in Bombay in street. There is no triangle but a multiage. I told you a pot of minestrone is there."

All students, this time, were very passionate and were listening and enthusiastic about the minestrone. Thus the philosophy class number 400 gets to the end with applause of the attending students.

THE HELL "JELL"

"Hello."

"Yes, hello."

"Mr. La' yé?"

I was a bit confused and waited for a moment to answer. Since "j" in Eastern Europe is pronounced "I", I replied "But!"

"Yes, we know, the second part of your name is Vardé."

"Not exactly, but what are you calling for anyway?"

"We call you from Hell. This is the operator."

For a moment I was almost in hell, and between two "vardi". The plural of "vardé" is "vardi" in Italian, and "La' yé" means between in Persian. So I must be lodged between two "vardi", and was sure that I was gonna be in Hell between my parents, who are, most surprisingly in Hell. Why?

I had hundreds of interpretations and justifications for this call. First of all, I don't know why the operator did not pronounce the "j" correctly. It was like "ee" or "y".

Second of all, was he really from Hell? Or is he working like a volunteer but originally from Heaven? May be he is the General operator for both Heaven and Hell.

I've got the answer. He might be from the old communist countries and God doesn't like the communism. That is why they are there. But he could have been there before the communist regime.

Another possibility is God doesn't like the letter "J" and He orders to change it into "ee". "No way" I said to myself. "Why should he? John, Jesus, Jacob and many other heavenly persons have names with "J". But wait a minute, all of them were tortured or crucified and or got martyred. Yes my man, God did not like the "J" in their name, that's why . . ."

"But look you're talking nonsense!" I said to myself, "and God is not acting like a child, right?" I shook my head and all of a sudden I had the answer: I said "Latinos".

The operator continues as my heart was beating above 911 times a minute!

He said "What?"

"Nothing", I replied. But again to myself I was saying "Latinos don't pronounce "J" and they have it for "h" or "ee". Yes, Hell's operator had a Latino's accent." God doesn't like them, right? These "illegal" immigrants who once were exterminated by heavenly Western European "Saviors", are back again with larger "testicles" for multiplication, this is the answer.

"What is the answer? Do you accept the collect call fees?"

"I do, I do." I said, "How much is it per minute?"

"Not too much."

I went back to my hypothesis. Maybe the letter "J" is sacred for God that's why he has it for Jerusalem, John-Paul, Joseph, Joshua, Judas, Jews, Judaism. But he doesn't like "J" when it's in "jungle"! "Thou shall destroy jungles". Is this one of the Ten Commandments? Nonsense. I am stupid but if God wants to say "J" what letter will he use? Oh ya, the letter "G"! He loves it. That's his initial "G". Also we have it in "gun", "George", "Great Britain", "Graham", "Gabriel" . . . Right?

The operator said "Right. So you accept the call?" "What's the fee?" I said.

"I told you, it's not too much, it's a local call."

"Local call? It's not a long distance call?"

"No, No." he replied. "Your miserable life as well as the miserable life of 90% of the people of the planet Earth is as bad as the Hell. That's why it's considered as a local call."

I was still thinking about the operator's accent. How come he knows the life of 90% of people on Earth? I was still arguing about the "J".

He said, "Listen. You'd better talk to our customers who want to talk to you and every moment is metered by our Angelic computer system."

"Is your system counting every minute as two minutes like our A.T.A.T.?"

"What?"

"Acceptable Torture by Armed Theocrats."

"What do you mean? One minute is one minute for you and a bit less for "more equal people".

"Here, one minute is two minutes and sometimes more."

"What the hell are you talking about?"

"Did you say you're calling from Hell?"

"Yes"

"But you seem a very reasonable person to me."

"Everybody is reasonable here."

"Why are they in Hell, though?"

"This is a matter of interpretation; to be reasonable is sometime a sin here."

He said "interpretation" and I went back to my name: "Lajevardi" and he was saying something like Layévardé. May or may not be me.

"Vardé" or "Verdi"? "Verdi" was the Italian opera writer and composer and "Lei" in Italian is "you" or "are you", in other words the operator wanted to say "Are you Verdi"?, a person of Verdi's family? But why is "Verdi" in Hell? Oh yes! May be God the Lord does not like opera and specially "Aida". That is why Verdi is in Hell, and he wants to talk to one of his family members? May be all Italians are in Hell. Because they have defeated the Greek who had hundred of gods and were very sophisticated people, with a good relation with" sky". That's why they killed god damned Socrates.

"No Mister, it can't be; it has to have another explanation which could be "lei verde", which means "are you Green"? I said to myself. "That's it. Greens, the Green party". God doesn't like them. They prevent the "good people" cutting trees to build temples, churches and mosques and of course corporations.

Yes! Yes! Yes! This is the good reason but why are they calling me? Oh yes. I used to teach "Ecology" for a while and . . . , but it has no sense to it. Why somebody from Hell would want to talk to me? May be they're preparing a lot for me there.

They operator came to my help and said "Are you still there?"

"Where?" I replied.

"I don't know where you should be; on or in the earth. I am not from there."

"Where are you from? You must be from another universe right?" I replied to figure out his country of origin.

"I don't know what you're talking about," he said.

"You have no idea about the Big Bang?" I said.

"Everything is big here. You know what I am talking about, right?"

"Yes of course, like in Texas, and everything is big there, even their leaders have a very big and unused brain."

"I don't know. They are not coming here, these guys. They have good connection and go straight to heaven."

Right, how silly I am? And what a damn question I am asking. The operator asked me in a soft voice "Do you know how many minutes passed by and you're still on your crazy questions?"

"You know, I am not sure you dialed the correct number," I said.

"Is this so and so your God damned number?"

"God!"

"No, I did not mean it. What I mean is your area code for the planet earth is 911, right?"

"Yes"

"And your country, your state, your city and ..."

"Are you using the CIA system? Which is Communicating Intergalactic Anti-human?"

"No God forbid. We have our own communication system which is relayed in Yamkaran near the holly city of Ghomus in Persia."

"You mean Jamkaran? (Where the Messiah will appear, according to Shi'ites).

"Yes."

"Everything looks like my phone number and almost my name, except

for the letter "j"."

"You know, like all other Iranians you'd better change your name otherwise inhabitants of Hell could easily tell your origin and they will not let you in peace at all. You know these rednecks are very fascist and prejudiced and they don't like triple A's."

"Triple A's?" I said.

"Yes. Arabs, Amigos and Africans."

"Yes, they have their own reason." I said. "They have built this magnificent Hell and they don't want immigrants to occupy and disturb it."

All of sudden from the other side of the line somebody called my name. "Nasser. Nasser Joon" (Dear Nasser with correct "J" pronunciation) With a face like stone and acting like a dead person, I managed to come back to myself and while I was shaking, I still got the name of my Lord on my lips and said "Mom!"

"Yes, your Dad is here too. Say hello to him."

"Hi Dad. Are you alone?"

"No everybody is here from stone throwers in Jerusalem to stoned adulterous women." said my Dad.

"I understand, but you don't deserve Hell."

"We obviously do my son." replied my mom. "God is fair, a very good judge, a very good believer in justice".

"How come? You always respected the ten commandments; you have never committed the seven deadly sins, the capital sins. You always respected all other religions. You always took care of the poor, you always paid respect to elders, you have taken care of needy people, you paid on time your tithe and your tax and even your credit cards. You have never polluted the environment. No car, no A/C, you have never done pee in stream of water or earth while walking, did you?"

"Stop it man, I am crying for them," said the operator.

"No my son, "said my mom, "but …"

"But what? What else, did you respect your parents? Your teachers? Of course you did. You've also respected your children. You did not drink alcohol. You did not do drugs. You gave away your assets to build schools for handicapped kids. You cosigned checks for your boss in order to save him and you both finished up in jail. What else your god damned God wanted? Why are you there?"

"Mind your language son," replied my mom. She had a strong voice when talking to her kids and her husband, and she continued "The issue is …"

I did not let her continue and sadly said, "Mom you used to have problems with hearing, right?"

"Yes."

"How come you are so good now?"

"Here we have the best doctors like Albert Schweitzer and all the best specialists."

"What are they doing there? Is God crazy? If they were so good why …"

"They are good, but they were bad for insurance and drug corporations. They did not charge the poor people, and did not prescribe enough medications, and finally they were just bad for the business. Besides good doctors we also have an implacable skilled Iranian who changed the heat into an A/C system here."

"Oh my!"

"Yes my son," said my dad, "We did not drink alcohol and we did not do drugs. That was bad. That was very bad for the business run by 'more equal' people, who are very equal with other people as they pretend in the media and entertainment corporations, but in reality they are a little bit 'more equal' than the others. So 'thou shall kill' if it's good for them. 'Thou shall do adultery' if they want to. Thou shall steal and lie for them if they get prosperous. So we did not commit any capital sins but we have committed whole lot of capitalism sins. We did not get divorced. Divorce is very good for increasing consumption and good for business of corporations. Besides that, you guys, our children, had also forgotten some essential funeral traditions."

"What?" I said anxiously. "What are you talking about?" I replied in a miserable tone.

"Your conversation is about to finish because of too many calls," said the operator.

"Operator, Sir, please let us to come to the conclusion," I said.

"OK, but remember, here everybody is Bishop, Rabi, Khakham or Ayatollah. Titles given by George of Great Britain."

I felt that his voice was unfriendly and snobbish.

"OK, OK, Mr. Khayatbishe."

"Mind your language, what is that?" He said.

"Nothing, to offend. Just the amalgam of the above titles since I don't know yours." Mt dad was laughing in the distance.

"Oh yeh? OK, but …" I continued my conversation with my parents.

My father said, "Are you sure that your insurance company will pay for the call."

"Yes. Of course. They're here for this," I said.

My mom said "No. They're not there for this. They are there to make you happy. Remember that, never argue with them. This would be a new capitalism sin which was recently declared by the Heaven. As a matter of fact this is the reason we called you, to get you aware before God sues you."

"What?" I said vigorously. "Capitalism sin?"

"Yes kid," replied my dad. "Whatever they say, you have to accept and obey and follow it. Don't argue. They're there to make you happy like your mom said."

"But," (I was about to explode), "What happiness? They're collecting our money and getting richer and richer without giving us any service. I go to my doc. He gives a diagnosis to show a severe and unstable illness in order to get more money out of the insurance company. With the diagnosis my premium gets higher and higher. For this new diagnosis they send me to get a MRI. The MRI comes with no positive sign of illness. The insurance company says "You don't have such an illness." and don't pay for the MRI. The only thing remaining is my higher premium and higher co-payment and MRI to pay for."

"That is great. You have to suffer in order to get to Heaven, and of course without arguing. If you are tortured, don't tell anybody. If you do, the Hell is waiting for you." said my mom.

This conversation was getting informative, especially when my father said

"Whenever you protest, there are some young frustrated persons who get awareness of their frustrations and they feel the lack of "fairness, "justice" and "good will" by their government. They will have had their eyes opened and see the government inclination and bias toward some beloved "more equal" people. Then these unhappy persons who have no place in Heaven and no human rights at all will generate violence. Then what? Obviously "you", you who argue and question are the cause of the violence."

"OK dad, I understand, now. The world is created for some who are "more equal". If they say to me" That donkey can go easily up on the firefighter's ladder and will extinguish the fire." I will say "Of course they can do it" and I will add "While on the ladder they can sing like mocking bird".

"This is my son!"

"But a good question for you guys, Did it happen you are in Hell because of these kind of things or what?"

"Oh Lord. That is not all. That was just one of our capitalism sins." said my dad.

"I know. The other is "to argue when the beloved more equal people are asking for your money, your life, your time and your services." You have to give it right away. Right?"

"Right," both replied.

"If I don't have it, what happens?" I said.

"If you don't have home or dinner on the table that is exactly what Heaven wants. If you have them give 'em to them. Start to eat bread and onion or bread and tree leaves, or soup of doggy poop full of proteins, minerals and especially vitamin S., vitamin H., vitamin I., and vitamin T., which are essential for poor people's body and mind. Sell you wife, daughter, kidney (or your testicles, "said my mom at the same time as my dad was continuing) in order to please the masters."

"Yes, yes I know. I have realized that I have to write papers and articles and give it to "more equal people" in order to please them, which means to please the Heaven. And I know, dad, you have published something without adding their name. What about the rest of the sins?"

My dad said "Yes, I have published a book which was about some food recipes which, in reality, turned out to be "their food"! And so I had no legitimacy in publishing that. Another book was about some ingredients which were so called "against their culture" so the book was taken out from the bookstore shelves. The book about the "property of foods" had the name changed and the author, then got published. Nothing for me, zip, when I've protested. That was it, your mom and I got in jail and tortured as terrorist and finally killed with "plutonium"."What? This is terrible! How about the freedom of speech, ban on torture, ban on radioactive materials?" "Ah, Ah, you're arguing my dear." said my mom.

"You have to cry when they want you to and how they want you to," said my dad.

"OK, OK, what else? Anything else?" I said.

"You remember my son. You got our dead bodies in 9-11 and you straight away sent us to the cemetery. You did not make up our face, and you did not put on us our nice garments and dresses." "So?" I said.

"So what? It's supposed to be done. It's good for the business and to fail doing so it's a capitalism sin." said my dad.

"Really? What about people who die in a plane crash?" I said.

"Yes, and after that you did not shake our body while in the grave!" continued my dad without paying attention to my argument. He continued 'Don't argue while I am talking, understand?"

"To shake the body in order to get rid of the small peaces of the soul" added my mom. "That is what I wanted you to remember."

"OK, then what?" I said darkly, with a down turned mouth, while shaking my head.

"Don't make that face," said my mom.

"What? Are you seeing me from that distance?" I said.

"You're not that far," said my dad.

With this sentence my mouth fell open and I started to look around me. I was scared and blew a couple of times into the air, like "poof," "poof."

From the other side the operator said something in a tenor voice. "Are you farting into the God Telecom?"

"No. Who are you?" I said it while my middle finger was up toward the sky.

"Don't worry son," said my mom. "God is not furious if you insult **him**. Don't insult his beloved "more equal" people and their corporations, otherwise you will be in Hell like all other poor people."

"I would not say "poor", I would say "stupid poor people"." said my dad.

I was listening and thinking. They were right, we did not shake them while putting them in the grave. We did not knock on the grave stone while reciting the "redeeming verses". This knocking is good to run off the "grave's interrogators". We did not give pizza and burgers to people who attended the funeral. That is a bad deed against food corporations; we did not offer them sacred drugs while singing the Gospel of "Let us destroy Babylon", of David.

So why do we expect to see them in someplace else than Hell?

POEMS

Oneness
By : Dr. N.S.L

Once upon a time, in the Eastern down,
There was but one number, the number one.
Who was dancing like a shining star.
Tango and Waltz, forgetting the old memoir.
Turning round, like a Sufi, on and on.
In tavern, on the dirt , and on the lawn.
The number one, the Substance of our " una".
Who gets the Sun's light on its " laguna".
Absorbe the Existance, like la " Luna".
Nothing but the one, the number one.
I become one with the "oneness".
My heart taking over my dumbness.
All my prejudice and ego disappeared, toneless.
The rest of the body has gone, but one.
I am in the Divine Bar,like a "Clochard".
What a sensation of oneness,with Almighty " Attar".
I am voiceless in junction to the number one.
I look around, nothing is left of me.
I am a dead branch, without Thee.
Just a glance at me , and you will see.
That I 'll be alive,not a Dead Sea.
Once upon a time,there was but one. The number one.

Pledge of Union.
The Echo of Uniting Souls.
BY: Dr. N.S. Lajevardi

O thou, my companion of flight.
Reply to my greeting "amourette".
Bring your Shadow to my sight.
O thou, the garden of my secret.
And my relievers of sufferance and regret.
Let us be the companion of Light,
To the Fontaine of Eternity and yet
Let us be a new lyric for the love
melody, new Sonnet.
If in the sky of this journey,
We feel the smell of dangers.
If throughout this journey,
A bullet comes from strangers.
If my lips are dry and bitter.
And recall my dusty desert and litter.
If my wings are cut and my feathers broken.
And my only guest is sufferance
and heart broken
If any existance sings the song of suppress.
Because of my fatigue and weakness.
If my glass is like emptiness of obscurity.
If my eyes are full of tears of insecurity.
If my silence is a tongue-tied involution.
To promote inner dryness and destitution
If my sigh burns my essence.
But my soul and my substance.
Will be still, retiring, from the mirror of selfishness.
Your generous hands' caresse,
Is the remedy of my grief and illness,
Place my head on your shoulder for consolation.
Let us be in the garden of Light.
The seal of Pledge and reconciliation.
Let us be in the Crest of perfection.
United and beloved for each other, a divine celebration

Paraphrase translation of a Rumi Sonnet (Ghazal)

Don't depart, come closer, don't be false and shy.
Praise the Lord Almighty in the Beauty of Sky.
Don't go away, from the Holy Dome.
The antidote is in the Holy Venom.
Come, reveal to the root of the root of thyself.
Molded of clay, yet a knead.
From the Certainty, your substance is the seed.
Of the Treasure of Holy Light, your creed.
Yet a melody of music of the Divine Reed.
Come, reveal to the root of the root of thyself.
Once you get freed of selflessness.
You'll be dragged from your ego and madness.
Away from traps, remorse and sadness.
Come, reveal to the root of the root of theyself.
Don't fix your sight too low.
How to be happy? with heavy sorrow?
With that "regarde" so full of flames of tomorrow?
Come, reveal to the root of the root of theyself.
You're born from grace of the Lord of nonaggression
And came here with a Ray of the Lord of Compassion.
A little drunk, but gentle, stealing our heart and passion.
Come, reveal to the root of the root of theyself.
Why suffer at the hand of things that tease?
Rejoice, you're not slave of disappointment seas.
You're a ruby embeded in granite, so please
Come, reveal to the root of the root of thyself.

Translation of Rumi's souls ' evolution By: N. S. L

I passed away from mineral state,
   to become " flora"
I passed away from vegetal state,
   to become " fauna"
I passed away the animalia,
   to become " persona",
No fear, of dying, not even a "faux pas"
I've never become less, in this process.
So, I may lift up my head wings and soar as "Cherubim"
And, I ought to jump from the Angel's stream.
Everything perishes, except his Supreme.
Once again, I'll be sacrificed from the Cherubim,
To become that, which cannot come into imagination
The Divine melodies will say with admiration.
Truly, truly, to Him, is our destination.

Translation of some Rumi's Rubaii

On the seeker's path
    Fool and Guide are the same.
On the love's path,
    Man of inside or outside are the same.
Who is offered the wine of the Union
    Will preach that "gnostic or agnostic" are the same

Do not come to us without tambourine
    For we "feste".
Rise and beat the drum
    For we're the Majesty.
We're drunk, but not by grap-wine substance
We're far away from what you 'be in mind and conscience.

Every day my heart laments in its suffering for thee.
While thy merciless heart is more hateful of me.
Thou left me alone, but thy suffering did not
Rightfully, thy suffering is more faithful than thee

Another Rumi's translation by N.S.L

Any Astus I played in your love was an illusion.
Any agony I felt, without you , was an illusion
There is no medecine, no remedy for this pain.
Who can cure me? For my pain is an illusion

Rūmi's Rubaï traduit en francais

La Porte de l'union est fermée par la bien-aimée.
Le Coeur blessé et brisé est aimé par la bien-aimée.
Dorénavant, moi et ce blessé a la porte de la bien-aimée.
Parceque le Coeur blessé est trés aimee par la bien-aimée.

Il mio Sonetto in French

"L' Orifice"
Tiens la fenêtre fermée, fermement.
La brise va briser le coeur de l' âme.
Ce froid, qui ne Previent nulement.
D'un départ déplorant.
El,Ce qui a cassé le dôme de mon âme.
Celui qui a volé mon coeur et mon humeur
Avait embrassé le cadavre de la douleur
Tiens ton coeur vivant par la force de l' intérieur.
Puisque, de la fenêtre et sa prefondeur.
Ne Pènétra que le chagrin et la douleur.
Cet orifice était fermé depuis l'éternité.
Il était fermé au dynamisime de ténébrosité.
Les fenêtres, helas, sont remplies de depressions.
Les orifices et le soucis se reconnaissent.
Les fenêtres seront mieux tenues fermées sans cesse.
La nuit de dehors brule la vie et la compréhension.

The opera of the Jungle

I am a black with a callus palm
Is it a condemnation?
I am a black who harbors in "ame".
My heart is a bloody jungle of miserable life.
Soaked in a bloody desire of promised wife.
I am a black, presumptuous "against love and sky.
Against the fairness, against the tie".
My companions now, gypsies of the nostalgic path of life.
The night is my confidant, on my site
My coeurus maid is a magpie of distressed night.
My music, the melody of exile and separation.
My ears, full of wrath, fear and exasperation.
My ancestors were from the necropolis of poverty and tribulation.
Each of them, one after one, "maestri" of Lamentation.
For the vessel of curse, enslavement and subjugation.

One by one, radiant and full of charm and lure.
Heart's ravishment, our allure.
Capturing the soul and belief of slave brokers.
Of the desert of tradesmen and slaver traffickrer.?
Merchants have an eye of appreciation.
On the king of Marsh, admiration.
We'll be selected one by one from hundred, still.
Men of profession, qualification, and trill.
Diligent, die hard, and tall like a cedar.
But still Chained on feet, roped hands, mouths closed, like a jar.
Claps arounds the faces, is it indulgence?
All these, so, as to not address my grievance
And secrets to other slaves, my intention
     would die in the cocoon.
Don't even talk to ghosts or to the moon
One by one on the ship of the owner.
What a dissension and variance.
On elbow a burning mark of contract, sheriff and order.
Like cattle's, my arms has a secret burned number.
This number graved on my leg, my pole.
As my name and identity.
So were me, and our being in brevity

Then few long hours on the deck of the ship, the haul.
For rowing, till we are out of breath.
Nobody comes to your help from the earth.
Then, after we buy the heaviness of water, the tides.
With our sacrifice price, our lives this side.

To bring the sail in the proper track.
You'll dance with bloody wind, with bloody, Wounds, attack.
Till death beating the door, the gate.
But still my feet chained, is a hidden secret Untold fate
Sometime from the extreme downcast fatigue and exhaustion.
Some will perish from the wave of storm, disruption.
Handsome owners, toss their corpse to the sea.
Feeding the sharks, how nice, and generous they can be.
Corpses are dancing with hurricane!!
Then, the ship and these brave slaves in pain.
Continue, their route, simple and brief.
This marine made in Cardiff.
Goes to the New world, with determination.
To erode the prairie of endegenous tribes.
For assembling an erotic marsh of prostitution.
Our ship, anchor at port, "Bonair".
With waves of traders with the yellow hair.
Then, each of us, sent to a merchant.
Slave broker stall.
How we made it to the merchant?
Limping and rising and still walking tall.
A merchant buys us and a new podlock.
Of enclosures, captivity and detention.
To my foot, my hand, my soul and my configuration.
Then order of "Go Go" to the untouched green forests flora
While singing the song of forsaken, lonesome.
I forgot the mystical Ballade of love and devotion

Our caravan continues, still, toward the forests, the jungle, diorama.
Which is so picturesque like an intoxicating tableau!
As though, in between leaves, the art of Picasso,
And from next den to the following hell.
Sudden, oh, listen, the voice of bugle.
And the trumpet of freedom, will be.
The resident of this residence, through the door.

Which verses like Abraham Psalms caresses ears.
Through the following, melody, no less no more.
"Oh you, slaves of disappointment sanctuary.
From now on, every body will get.
This is our pledge.
A star from sky. However, don't forget.
For the generation who is the decoration of the world secret.
The adorned, people, the chosen one, yet.
Will have the privilege.
We will add, then a galaxy for each of them, no regret.
And in the dawn of freedom, everybody, then.
Will have a moon and star as gift of heaven.
When the dust of the night is settled.
And tenebrity is over in the mountain.
We put your gift in your pocket."
But we don't have pocket in our pocket.
Our "robe" is made of pockets.
It is pocket by pocket and the gift is in the bottom of our pockets.
And in a eyes blink, at a glance.
The handsome men of the city of romance.
Self-chosen-the-best, self-chosen-governance.
Cut our pricy pockets.
And transformed it into priceless pockets.
And at its place, they put a leaden star.
Oh yeah, in the city of the people of providence.
Then strange things happened, while they were shouting.
"these ignorant slaves."
Have robbed our moon and sun", oh ya!
Then every body of populace, then after, every hours.
Had a mean like look at robbed slaves.
The mean look of them stares at our feet, once again.
We were petals harvested down like wheat winnowed, once again.
Shing stars? That was added Satiric to world history.
That was a lesson of illusion, a blow on the mouth.
For us a happy ending? Are you kidding?
No way, don't even imagine.
Why the horizon should be clear? why? No way.
Expect the war, with the satan, no other way.
My soul and body are in Chagrin.
For "non-existence" is certain.
To happen, to call.

The autumn is there, I am ready for fall!
This is being and nothingness.
The first one for them and nothingness for us.
What is washing my brain is now crushing, you know.
Heavier than sledge and hammer, rocks to and fro.
And worse than prison, all day.
Like culturless prostitutes, I should say.
Libertine, vagrant, ethicless and rootless.
Our enjoyment , our bosses says:
"Should be narcotics, liqueurs and christal.
Which is in the ambuscade, enough for all
Then, the boss says; transfer him from a jail to a prison
And from a prison to this headstock."
And from this bed, to an ashy bed, a new captivity.
That is the way how the royal court, the divinity.
Of justice is celebrated in a jungle of wild loneliness.
From a lord to another invisible owner, new holiness.
Oh thou the charming girl of lost light.
We were searching for the twilight of destiny.
Or destiny's delicate twilight.
We lay together in the sultry night.
From some invisible moon beams crept.
Into the anywhere, where, we slept.
Here finally, we've found that.
We don't belong to this small earth.
Starving on this careless soil that.
Gave us, all as a colored birth
You were in my bed, the fountain of generosity
Oh thou, of the same tribe of despair and unfortunate disgraced.
Who lost her moon and stars, how strange?
Hidden and sleeping, in the pocket of imposture.
Thou, who are from the family of no hypocrisy
And family of pure nature and spirit.
Who has never gotten the light of reception
Or spouse in her spirit
Listen, I am the same nice black with good
Statures of the monastery of deception.
Who was the white line of chalk, sketched.
With an air and had been sedentary.
Oh the wall of the dishonored city and borough.
And recites and sings poems and fables of sorrow.

From his regrets, desires, and his glories.
Has his own unfulfilled aspirations and so many stories.
O thou charming girls of the tavern of tenebrity.
Here, I am, the same handsome, sweet , pity.
Good looking man with soul so dead.
Who never has dreamed and said.
"This is my own, my native land.
Whose teacher is in foreing strand"
You were like me, searching door to door your star.
And we were so happy and of wonderful ship so bizarre.
All the night, tired, cold and hungry was I.
And owl's cry, of the heaviness of my sigh
What a melancholic cry.
This is a black man's story and lullaby.